stages | episode one

GRETEL PARK PUBLISHING
gretelpark.com

stages | episode one

a sophie walker novella

katie paul

GRETEL PARK PUBLISHING • SYDNEY

CHAPTER ONE

The room, draped in black plastic, reminded Sophie of a scene from an episode of *Dexter*. But the shiny covering wasn't there to protect the walls from blood and tissue, but from the orange smears of fake tan. Sophie shivered as Pip painted the last coat of brown on her body, feeling the cold liquid run in dribbles down the back of her thighs. In the florescent light of the dressing room, the tanning solution made her skin seem dirty, as though she had bathed in a muddy creek. The colour had caked around the outside edges of her nails and tinted her French manicure a pale yellow, making her fingers look like those of a pack-a-day smoker.

'Turn around,' said Pip, 'I'll fix your suit.'

Pip drew two lines of glue along the edges of Sophie's backside and pressed the green lycra of Sophie's bikini against the trail of sticky liquid.

'Face me and let's have a proper look at you,' said Pip. She stood back and surveyed Sophie's body. She bit her lip. 'Have you got tape?'

'In my bag,' said Sophie.

'Fold over the skin on your belly,' said Pip, 'I'll tape it down.'

Sophie pinched together the papery thin skin on her belly, until it resembled a puckered appendix scar. Pip covered the seam of flesh with a line of brown Elastoplast and glued the front of Sophie's bikini pants over the top. A mess of white stretch marks intersected across Sophie's hips. Fake tan couldn't completely cover everything.

Sophie looked around for a clock on the wall, but if there had been one, it was now covered by black plastic. The only thing visible was a wall of mirrors, currently obscured by a cluster of girls admiring their reflection. She tried to determine who else might be in the Master's division, but the lack of fat on the other women's faces made them all look older than their years.

'How long do we have?' she asked.

Pip looked at her watch. 'About fifteen minutes,' she said. 'It's time to pump up.' She handed Sophie two eight-kilo dumbbells. 'Lots of reps.'

As Sophie curled the dumbbells, her tongue stuck to the roof of her mouth. All she wanted in that moment was a cold can of Diet Coke but she hadn't been able to drink any for the past four days. The carbonated beverage had been eliminated to prevent bloating. Instead of Diet Coke, Sophie had been drinking water — a litre every hour for the past two days. She was glad she had taken time off work because she had been permanently in the bathroom. Yesterday, when she had caught a train to Burwood to register for the competition, she had needed to pee at the train station. The women's toilets were busy so she had been forced to use the men's. A water-loaded bladder waited for no one. Eight hours ago Sophie had stopped drinking anything at all. Dehydration was essential for maximum definition. At least being this parched reduced the need to go to the toilet before she went on stage. She was looking forward to a drink.

'Any word from Megan?' she asked.

'She hasn't called since this morning,' said Pip. 'You'll be fine. We've done everything on the list.'

Megan, Sophie's coach, had left Sophie a list of what to take and what to avoid. Sodium depletion to reduce cellular fluid, potassium tablets to prevent cramping, and carbohydrates to swell her muscles. Sophie had even had colonic irrigation the day before to guarantee a flat stomach. Megan hadn't been able to make the competition because she was attending her niece's christening. Although Sophie felt a little deserted by her coach, she was glad to have Pip, an Italian beauty, dark haired and perfectly proportioned, who had won the Queensland title the year before.

A loud clear voice cut through the river of chatter. 'Masters Figure Ladies,' the young woman announced, 'please line up at the bottom of the stairs.'

Sophie took a moment to consider the woman running the show. Normally, it was Sophie who was in charge so it felt disconcerting to be on the other side. She had never sought out the lime-light, preferring to stay in the darkness on the side of the stage, calling instructions like an orchestral conductor to her reclusive lighting, sound and staging operators. It struck her, not for the first time, how agreeing to stand on stage in nothing more than a crystal encrusted bikini, like some faded pageant queen, was totally out of character. But a body-building competition was the ultimate challenge. Once she had told everyone at work she was going to be competing and had engaged a trainer, there was no turning back. The early morning ninety minute sessions in the gym, the six meals a day, the tuna, the chicken breasts, the protein powder, the steamed green vegetables had all been worth it. The pain of forcing her body to lift heavier and heavier weights, running kilometres on the treadmill and the ever present irritation of hunger were easier to bear than the shame of failure. In four months, she had lost six kilos, gram by gram, and had reduced her body fat to twelve percent. All her efforts had led her to this morning when she had stood on the scales and seen the smallest number she had ever seen. Now, here in some sports centre in a suburb she had never heard of, her hard work and discipline would be displayed for the world to see.

Six women gathered at the base of the stairs, all taller, leaner and prettier than Sophie. Tears welled up in Sophie's eyes.

'Oh my God,' she whispered. 'I don't have a chance.'

'Stop worrying about them,' said Pip. 'This is about you. You've worked hard and you look amazing.' Pip safety-pinned a badge showing a large number five to the right-hand side of Sophie's bikini.

Sophie put the dumbbells down and bent over to put on her shoes. 'Stripper shoes' is what Pip called them — silver and plastic platform mules with six inch stiletto heels. Sophie had worn them around the house for months so she could walk in them with any kind of skill. The years of wearing work boots every day had made her arches and ankles unfamiliar with anything with a heel.

'Are these the right shoes?' asked Sophie. Panic gnawed at her growling stomach. 'They don't fit.'

'Your feet have shrunk,' said Pip, laughing. 'It's the dehydration.'

Pip held up a small hand mirror. Sophie checked her teeth for lipstick and ran her fingers through her short blond hair. The false eyelashes felt heavy and prickly on her eyes.

'Off you go,' said Pip. 'You look beautiful.'

Sophie's legs started to shake as soon as she walked up the stairs and continued to tremble as she stood in the wings.

'Competitor number five,' said the man standing at the podium. 'Sophie Walker.'

Sophie walked out onto the stage, pressing her feet into her shoes to prevent them from slipping. The applause was thin and weak. She smiled the exaggerated smile of a performer, showing her freshly whitened teeth to the few hundred people in the audience. A couple of people in the front two rows looked up at her, but a large percentage of the audience didn't stop talking, eating, moving between the seats, or checking the schedule. In the front row, a trestle-table had been set up, and behind it sat three judges. The first was a male body-builder, his steroid-enhanced shoulders and biceps bulging from underneath his singlet. He leaned back in his chair and yawned. The second judge was a peroxide blond woman with hard round breasts and diamonds on her fingers. The third man wore a suit and had his head bowed over a notebook in which he wrote furiously.

Sophie stood with one hand on her hip, her weight

on one leg. At posing class they had called it 'relaxed pose'. She didn't feel relaxed.

The female judge picked up a microphone. 'Symmetry round,' she said.

Sophie placed her feet together, her arms at her sides and faced the front. She clenched her muscles and sucked in her stomach.

'Turn to the right ... to the back ... to the left ... back to the front.'

The lights bearing down on Sophie were hot and bright, bleaching the colour from her skin and the striations from her limbs. Whoever had designed the lights had no idea how to flatter the human body. Dancers were never lit from above, but instead from the side, where the beams of cross-light left deep shadows, which separated muscle from bone, veins from flesh. Sweat started to bead on Sophie's top lip.

'Compulsory poses,' said the judge. 'Front double bicep.'

Sophie struck each pose as it was called.   Side chest, side triceps, rear double bicep, abdomen and thighs. Her left calf muscle cramped into a hard knot of pain. She pushed down on her heel trying to find relief, but the pain spread down to her toes. She smiled harder to cover the discomfort.

'Number nineteen, thirty-two and eight,' said the blond woman. Three girls walked to the front of the stage. As they posed again for the judges to determine who would win first, second and third, Sophie watched, envying the finalists their perfect shape. They all had wide shoulders with deltoid caps, sinewed thighs and roped calves. Sophie had none of those things.

She had anticipated that standing on stage would bring with it a profound sense of pride and accomplishment but all she felt was foolish. It was ridiculous to believe she had any chance of winning a place in this competition. Her natural shape was curved and round, and even at her leanest, her hips and thighs were more suited to child-bearing than the cover of *Oxygen* magazine. She had been deluded to imagine she could outrun her genetic inheritance.

A man in a t-shirt with *Australian Natural Body Building* printed on the chest stood in front the judge's table and handed around a box of pizza. The smell of grilled cheese and caramelised onion drifted up onto the stage causing Sophie's stomach to lurch with hunger. The two men took a slice each but the blond woman waved it away. She handed a slip of paper to the compere who returned to his position behind the podium.

'First place goes to ... competitor number eight,' said the compere, after he had announced number nineteen had placed third. A pocket of people on the left side of the auditorium erupted into cheers. Number eight, a tall, olive-skinned woman in a blue bikini, smiled and flexed her biceps. Number thirty-two looked disappointed to have only managed second place.

The compere handed the winner a plastic trophy and a tub of protein powder. As she walked off stage, she flipped her dark hair over her shoulder. 'I'm fifty-two,' she said to no one in particular. 'Fifty-two.'

Sophie was forty-five. She felt much older.

Back in the dressing room, Pip's eyes were glowing.

'I took some great photos,' she said. She held the digital camera so Sophie could see the small LCD screen on the back. 'Look.'

'Later,' said Sophie. She kicked off her shoes. 'First, get this outfit off me.'

Sophie stood in the shower and watched the stained brown water flow over the bottom of the bathtub and disappear down the drain. She pulled the band of Elastoplast from her belly and watched her skin expand. A dark bruise had formed over the creased skin, as though someone had punched her in the stomach. The house was silent and still. She hadn't known what time she would be home so she couldn't expect Michael to be waiting for her. She considered phoning him, but decided against it. She didn't want him to think she was checking up on him.

After her shower, she dressed in a pair of tracksuit pants and a sweatshirt, and headed to the kitchen. A portion of grilled chicken breast sat dry and tinged with grey in the refrigerator. She fought the urge to pick up the phone and order pizza. Both Megan and Pip had warned her about post-competition binging. Sixteen weeks of hard work could be undone in a matter of days, especially now she had stopped taking diuretics. She heated the chicken in the microwave and ate it in front of the computer. Izzy, Sophie and Michael's tortoiseshell cat, curled into a ball at her feet.

I didn't win, but I had a good time, she wrote on Facebook and posted one of the photos Pip had emailed through, but not before she had photoshopped the cellulite from her thighs and the dark smudges from around her eyes.

The responses flooded in. *Congratulations. You look awesome*, the messages read. She clicked LIKE as each one appeared below her photo. No one would say anything else, would they?

In the bathroom, she slid the scales over to their optimum spot on the tiles (two squares out from the toilet and four squares in from the bathtub.) As she took off her sweatshirt, Izzy sauntered into the bathroom and looked up at Sophie with yellow eyes full of expectation. Sophie opened the back door and let the cat out.

Back in the bathroom, Sophie stripped off, leaving all her clothes on the floor. The scales lay waiting to pronounce their verdict. The digital readout danced momentarily before settling on 0.0. She stepped on and held her breath as the numbers counted up, wavered for a moment as if seeking some outside guidance, and then settled on the number that would determine how the next day would proceed.

Two kilos heavier than this morning. Two fucking kilos. Tears pricked at the corners of her eyes. Something must be wrong with the scales. She stepped off, adjusted their position, pushed the reset button, and waited for zero. She stepped on again, easing her weight onto the scales as gently as she could. The exact same number. Losing weight was like trying to contain a rabid dog — as soon as you turned your back, the animal would escape. She pushed the scales back into the corner and went to bed. After a few pages of her novel, her eyelids grew heavy.

The sound of Michael fumbling around in the dark trying to find the switch for the fan woke Sophie up. He couldn't sleep without the whirring noise in the background. The bed shifted underneath his weight as he lay down. Sophie smelled beer on his breath and stale sweat on his body. He settled with his back towards her, as far away from his wife as possible in the queen-sized bed.

'Aren't you going to ask me how I went?' Sophie asked, after a few minutes of silence.

Michael sighed. 'Did you win?'

Sophie rolled over to face the wall. Light from the street painted narrow strips of yellow around the edges of the blind.

'No,' she said.

'So you weren't good enough.'

'It was my first time and most of the women in the Masters' division have been training their whole lives. It takes years to get that kind of muscle size. Next time I'll have to build more muscle and get leaner.'

'I wouldn't bother if I were you,' said Michael, 'I prefer it when you're fat.'

Sophie felt her face grow hot, the flush travelling down her neck. In the silence she heard his breath thicken as he fell asleep. Only then did she allow the tears to spill onto her cheeks. When had Michael thought she was fat? When she had met him seventeen years ago, she was only a size twelve. It wasn't until her forties that she had started to need a size fourteen. When she could no longer zip up her jeans, she had gone on a diet. The same diet that had eventually led her to competing. When was it that she was the kind of fat Michael preferred? Was it during their courtship, or perhaps their early days of marriage? He didn't seem to enjoy this tiny, streamlined version of herself — he hadn't touched her in months. Longer than months. But they weren't any different from any other couple who had been married for years. It was normal that passion died. To be honest, she didn't even miss it. It might have had something to do with not menstruating any longer, but she didn't give it much thought. She was simply glad to be rid of the monthly inconvenience and the sensation of Michael's damp sweaty hands on her skin.

Sophie arrived first for the six a.m. Monday morning spin class wearing a grey baseball cap to disguise her dishevelled hair. After draping her towel over the handlebars of a bike in the front row and placing her water bottle in the cradle, she went to the bathroom. She put her arm underneath the tap and scrubbed at a stripe of dark brown tanning solution that ran the length of her forearm.

By the time the class was finished, her top was soaked through with sweat. Her backside ached where her tail bone had pressed against the hard bicycle seat. In the change room, she wrapped herself in an over-sized jumper and a big woollen overcoat to protect her from the cold outside. Spring seemed reluctant to arrive that year. It was October, but the mornings were still chilly. She sometimes thought she only had enough energy to make it home because of the bottle of energy drink she bought on the way out. Sophie believed in cardio on an empty stomach. She couldn't have breakfast until she had earned it.

Sophie put a dessert bowl on the kitchen scales and reset the dial to zero. She spooned in 50g of rolled oats and tipped them into a pot of boiling water. Then she measured out 30g of protein powder and 30g of psyllium husk, ready to add to her porridge once it had cooked. As the pot of oats simmered on the stove, Sophie went to the computer under the window in the lounge room and checked her emails. Outside, as the dawn nudged the darkness from the sky, she noticed the garden looked different. Where once were empty stretches of soil, there were now small bushes and larger shrubs. There was even her favourite tree, a frangipani, planted in the corner. The pavers had been swept clean and the loose bricks stacked into an orderly pile.

Sophie crept into the bedroom. 'Sweetheart,' she said, touching her husband on the shoulder. 'Have you been gardening?'

Michael propped himself up on one elbow, blinking sleepiness from his eyes. 'Yeah,' he said. 'I did it while you were away yesterday.'

'It looks incredible,' she said. 'I'm sorry I didn't notice sooner. Thank you.'

'It was meant to be a present for making it to the competition. But it looks like shit.'

'No it doesn't, it looks so much better than it did before. I love it.'

'Don't get carried away,' he said. 'It's just a few plants jammed into the dirt.'

She kissed him on the forehead, his skin damp against her lips. 'Thank you.'

He shifted away from her and laid down. 'Shut the door on the way out,' he said. He pulled the pillow over his head.

'I'll be leaving in an hour,' she said. 'I'll see you in a couple of weeks.'

'Bye. Now shut the door.'

CHAPTER TWO

A good-looking man opened an old wooden door and held out his hand.

'I'm James,' he said. 'Production manager. Can I help you with your case?' His voice had an American accent. A dark mole showed through the salt-and-pepper stubble on his upper lip.

'No, it's fine,' said Sophie, as she shook his hand. 'Just show me where I can leave it until tonight.'

With the suitcase stowed in the corner of the kitchen, James led Sophie into the rehearsal room. It was a large room with a scuffed timber floor and posters of old theatre productions on the walls. There were racks of costumes on one side of the room and a props table covered in papers, guns and crockery on the other. At a long trestle table near the door, sat the director. He stood up, revealing a tall, thin frame. His hands were soft with polished fingernails, his handshake limp and yielding.

'Thanks for coming at such short notice,' he said. 'Our last stage manager...'

'...had to go back to Malaysia unexpectedly,' said James. The director gazed at him and then nodded.

'I'm Kim Chen,' the director continued, 'and this is my assistant Marco.' A small muscled youth smiled at Sophie with white teeth. 'The cast should be here in a minute,' said Kim Chen, 'then we'll get started.'

Sophie had read the script on the plane on the way down so she knew the production had a cast of only three — two males and a female. *Fault Lines*, imported from Malaysia for the Melbourne Festival, was a combination of dance, theatre and video. Technically challenging at the best of times, it would be almost impossible to learn in just a week. When the Festival organisers had rung to ask Sophie to recommend a stage manager to fill in at the last minute, she couldn't think of anyone available who would be up to the task. Sophie's boss, Greg, a great supporter of professional development, had agreed for Sophie to come down at short notice.

By the end of the day, Sophie's brain was filled with strains of discordant music and images of Gobo, a Japanese man, dressed as a traditional Geisha, his feet covered in white tabi inside wooden sandals. Julian, a blond Scandinavian, had rehearsed in nothing more than khaki canvas pants in the chilly hall, and had danced without ever tiring from what seemed to be a well of primal energy fuelled by the unrelenting beat of drums. Lissa, an exotic African American, provided the connection between the two worlds with her poetic monologues and interaction with the archival video footage. The show seemed to be about war, and memory, and gender, and bodies. Sophie didn't understand entirely what it meant but didn't have to. More than once she had been moved to tears during the day. It was a work which should be felt rather than analysed.

'I'll take you to the hotel,' said James, once they had tidied the rehearsal room and everyone else had left for the day. 'You're on the same floor as me.'

James insisted he wheel her suitcase during the five minute walk to the hotel. She was too tired to argue.

'I'm from Texas,' he told her. 'I met Kim Chen at an after party in New York.' He pushed open the door to her room and deposited the suitcase in the bedroom. 'This is my first time in Australia.'

Sophie was pleased to discover she had an apartment with a self-contained kitchen and a balcony overlooking the street. James stood in the entrance way, his hands in his pockets.

'What are you doing for dinner?' he asked.

'I'll grab something from the supermarket,' she said. 'I'm too tired to go out.'

James frowned for a moment before his face dissolved into a smile, his brown eyes dancing in the lamp light. 'I'm in Apartment 36 if you need anything,' he said. 'Just down the corridor.'

The supermarket was a small IGA with narrow aisles and two checkouts. The front of the store was filled with alcohol. Sophie hadn't drunk anything for a long time. Too many empty calories in a glass of wine. She inspected the trays of chicken in the fridge, the meat slimy and uninviting.

She was away from home, just one day out from competing, surely she deserved the night off?

Hoping no one would pay attention to what she was buying, Sophie filled her basket with all the things she had denied herself for the past four months. She started with a packet of six croissants, some ham and cheese, and then added a family block of caramello chocolate and a tub of vanilla ice cream. To be sure she had more than one thing to choose from for dessert, she also selected a bag of licorice and a bag of marshmallows from the lolly aisle. The loaf of bread and the tub of butter were for breakfast. She was sick of porridge.

Back in the apartment, Sophie only intended to eat two croissants and a small scoop of ice cream with a few squares of chocolate and a couple of marshmallows. She put everything else in the fridge, hoping if she couldn't see it on the bench she wouldn't be tempted.

The first bite of buttery pastry, salty ham and sharp cheese set her taste buds reeling. A strange wave of sensuality coated her brain, dissipating the anxiety left over from her day. The sensation felt like sliding naked into a bed of smooth satin sheets, relieving an ache that emanated not from a single location in her body but from the entire space around her. If she had believed in auras, she might have expected hers to have gone from the colour of bitumen to deep pulsing red. Nothing else felt this good.

She had heard of people starting to eat and waking up hours later surrounded by dirty dishes and empty wrappers, but Sophie never zoned out. She knew what she was doing. She ignored the voice in her head that kept screaming for her to stop. The sensation in her stomach that signalled she was full had been left dormant for so long that she no longer recognised it. She kept on eating until all the croissants were gone, until the bags of lollies were empty. When the squares of chocolate grew too sweet, she switched to raisin toast with butter. She stopped when she realised another mouthful would make her vomit. She had never gone that far. Only bulimics threw up.

When she looked down at her stomach bulging out over the top of her trousers she felt disgusted. This was the last time she would binge. Starting tomorrow she would go back to her diet, recording the calorie content of everything she put in her mouth. She set her alarm for five a.m. and laid out her leggings, sports bra, heart rate monitor and sneakers for the morning. Thank goodness the apartment complex had its own gym. She hoped there wouldn't be anyone there to witness her swollen legs and puffed face. If she couldn't take the laxatives she usually relied on in times like these because she couldn't afford to be in the bathroom all the next day, at least she could run for an hour and undo some of the damage.

Lying on the bottom of her suitcase were her scales. She carried them into the bathroom and placed them under the vanity unit. She decided not to step on them before she went to bed. She knew better than that.

The stage was black except for a pool of yellow light in the centre. Out in the darkened auditorium, Kim Chen sat at a long table fitted over the seats, his head bowed over a stack of papers. The light radiating from a desk lamp reflected off his black hair. Sophie sat next to him listening to him breathing over his headset microphone.

Kim Chen banged his hand on the desk. 'I'm still waiting for the fucking video,' he shouted. His microphone was still live. Sophie pulled her headset away from her ears.

James walked into the circle of light in the middle of the stage. Blue backlight created a halo around his head and shoulders. He was as handsome as any actor or dancer. He put his hand to the square metal box on his belt and pushed the talk button.

'We're working on it,' he said. He gestured towards the dark space in the grid above the stage. 'We're checking the bulb in the projector.'

'Shall we move to the next cue and come back?' asked Sophie. They had been in the theatre for almost two hours and were still working on the opening sequence. If they had any hope of getting through all the lighting, sound and video cues by the end of the day, they would have to keep moving.

'I have to see everything,' said Kim Chen. 'I don't know what it looks like if nothing is working. Are these people stupid?'

Sophie flinched. The men and women who worked in arts venues could be easily put off side. If they were on your side, they would do anything in their power to help you. But if you made them your enemy, they would make your life hell.

'It won't be long,' said Sophie, not having any idea how long it would take. She knew better than to ask what had gone wrong and how long it would take to fix it. Both questions just made the problem worse. Theatre technicians fixed things as quickly as they could. When something didn't work it was embarrassing for everyone. The problem would be solved without the interference of Sophie or Kim Chen.

'Why don't you go and grab a coffee?' she said to Kim Chen. 'I'll call you when we're ready. Alan — could we have work lights on stage and the house lights at half.'

The big overhead flood lights on the stage snapped on and florescent tubes in the wings and in the grid blinked awake. Kim Chen grunted as he put his headset on the desk. He pushed through one of the auditorium side doors and out into daylight.

'Can I grab a ciggy?' asked Alan's voice in her ear. He operated the lights from a glass booth at the rear of the balcony. 'I'll only be five minutes.'

'Of course,' said Sophie. 'Let me know when you're back.'

She rose from the desk and leaned into the pain in her hip. Her headset was wireless so she left it on her head. She walked down carpeted stairs in the auditorium and up wooden stairs to the stage. People were moving along the catwalk in the grid. In their black clothes, they seemed almost like ghosts with disembodied voices. James stood next to the Stage Manager's desk. Prompt corner it was called, on the left side of the stage from a performer's point of view. She would move to this position for the first Dress Rehearsal. Sometimes Stage Managers called shows from the lighting operator's position in the control room out the front, but Sophie liked to be near the action on stage.

'Is he always like that,' asked Sophie, 'or is this a bad day?'

James shrugged. 'Pretty normal,' he said. 'Wait till I tell him the blue sculpture piece for Act Three was damaged in transit. He's going to go ballistic.'

'How bad is it?' Sophie ran her fingers over the

smooth buttons on the Stage Manager's desk's console. The most important ones controlled her communication system so she didn't need to fiddle with buttons on her belt pack.

'There's a big dent on the back. Luckily it's on the upstage side so the audience won't see it. Roger's trying to patch it up in the workshop. It's either going to disguise the problem or make it worse.'

James stopped talking and cocked his head as though he were listening to a song playing in another room. Sophie couldn't hear anything.

'Here we go,' he said. He pointed to a space above his head. Sophie could see a small red flashing light. 'Are we good, Nick?' he called into the grid.

'Yeah, mate,' said Nick. 'A few seconds to reset and we're golden.'

'I'm back,' said Alan's voice over Sophie's headset. 'Shall I take out the workers?'

Sophie checked her microphone was still switched off and called out across the stage. 'Workers going out.' Into her microphone she said, 'Thanks Alan, let's go back to LXQ 14, but leave the houselights up until Kim Chen gets back.'

She pushed a button on the console and switched from talking on the show loop to the PA system backstage.

'Mr Chen, this is your call to the auditorium. Mr Chen, your call to return to the auditorium.'

Her fingers pushed another button. 'Nick,' she said, once more on the show loop. 'Can I have AVQ 1 paused up on the screen, please.'

When Kim Chen was seated back at the table, Sophie walked into the auditorium and resumed her place next to the director. A few moments after she was settled the house lights faded to black.

'I have an idea,' said Kim Chen, leaning towards her. 'What if we had actual rain falling in the last scene where Gobo loses his mind?'

'I'll look into it,' said Sophie. She knew the answer would be no. Gobo's kimono, his own possession, was too delicate and valuable to get wet. Plus neither he nor Julian would be able to dance safely on a wet floor. But Sophie rarely said no to a director at the first request. Sometimes they changed their mind about outrageous ideas without her saying anything, and sometimes they forgot all about it, usually when they were rushing to get through the original show without any modifications. On the rare occasions when she did say no, she always quoted someone else's expert opinion — an actor, the production manager, the head mechanist, the venue manager or the safety officer. She let her directors believe crazy requests were at least possible. She didn't want to block their creative ideas.

'Can you get James back on stage?' asked Kim Chen. He put his headset back on.

'James,' said Sophie, into her microphone. 'Can you come back on stage for a few minutes, please?'

'Anything for you,' said James. He slipped out of the darkness into the pool of light. 'What can I do for you?'

'Nothing,' said Kim Chen. 'I just enjoy looking at you.' They all laughed. 'You can go now.'

Sophie smiled. 'Nick, please standby to run the video,' she said.

'Standing by.'

'OK folks, let's get this show on the road.' She took a deep breath. 'AVQ 1 — GO.'

'**House lights and** workers — GO,' said Sophie. She leaned back against the cloth seat and watched the theatre transform from a mystical dream world into a working space with walls made of canvas and tape marks on the floor. 'Thank you everyone, that's it. Your next call is 10 a.m. on Monday morning. Have a good day off. Goodnight.'

She took off her headset and ruffled her hair where the headband had flattened it. The clock in the task bar at the bottom of Kim Chen's laptop read 10:17 p.m. She yawned.

James approached the desk. 'I'll come in early on Monday and move the side masking flats downstage,' he said. 'Aside from that, are you happy with everything, Kim Chen?'

'Yes.' Kim Chen slung his satchel over his shoulder. 'It's all looking gorgeous.'

James looked at Sophie and winked. He hadn't had to mention the repair to the blue sculpture piece. The head mechanist, Roger had filled and painted the gash so expertly that it was impossible to tell where the blemish had been.

'Soph,' said James, as Kim Chen walked out, 'you were incredible today. You have to let me buy you a drink.'

Sophie's first instinct was to say no, but she hesitated. She hadn't had dinner so she had room in her calorie allowance for one drink. The thought of the soft warm buzz of alcohol and some interesting conversation was enticing.

'Okay then,' she said, smiling. 'Just one.' As she closed the folder with her script inside, her engagement ring flashed. She wondered what Michael would think about her going out for a drink with another man. She hadn't spoken to her husband since she had left Sydney six days ago. He hated the phone. 'I'll only call if there's a problem,' he had said. She had sent him a text to say she was enjoying herself but had only received a one word response. Not talking to each other while she was away was a habit they had developed back before there were mobile phones, when long-distance calls from motel rooms were expensive. In those early days, Sophie was much more social with her work colleagues.

She had developed her first crush during the first year of her marriage, when she had been an Assistant Stage Manager on a tour of *Blithe Spirit* around regional New South Wales. Phillip, the Stage Manager, was ten years older than her, red-haired and wore a scruffy ginger beard. It certainly wasn't his looks she was attracted to. One night, when she was setting up the props for Act Two on stage during interval, Phillip had walked out wearing a pair of sunglasses and had started pointing at things. Sophie had to stop herself giggling in front of the audience.

'What was that all about?' she asked when they came off stage.

'I was pretending to tell you what to do,' he said. 'You're so efficient you don't even need me. I was asserting my male superiority...' He grinned. '... and failing miserably.'

They spent hours after the shows drinking rum and Coke in Phillip's room, usually accompanied by Tom, a TV actor from *Neighbours*, and Tom's partner Joseph. On Saturday afternoons, in between the matinee and the evening show, Phillip would take her to the TAB and teach her how to bet on the horses. He was an expert on horse racing — he even owned a racehorse himself. During that tour, Sophie found herself doing the things she would later come to recognise as danger signs — applying mascara, favouring dresses over jeans, and wearing dangly earrings and bracelets — she was preening. Nothing happened on that tour, or on any other. Sophie had always been faithful to her husband but she wondered if he suspected her of flirting when she was away. Where was the line between harmless and hurtful? Sophie had no idea how Michael felt. The subject of other men never came up. It was one more thing they didn't talk about.

'I'll meet you at Stage Door,' said James. 'I need to drop off the keys.'

The *Melbourne Supper* Club was plush and intimate with deep upholstered chairs and antique standard lamps. People spoke in hushed voices. The women in the room wore sequined dresses and diamond necklaces. Sophie felt plain in her black jeans and t-shirt. She shuddered as she took the first mouthful of wine, the smooth liquid feeling bitter on her tongue.

'I was beginning to think you didn't like me,' said James. He took off his jacket and laid it across the arm of the chair.

'Of course I like you,' said Sophie, feeling her cheeks grow warm. 'I'm not much of drinker.'

'Don't you ever go out?'

'Not to clubs or bars. Just the gym.'

'When?'

'Early mornings. It's usually the quietest.'

'Most theatre people are night owls. You're the first person I've met who willingly gets out of bed before lunch time.'

'I have to,' said Sophie, 'I have no choice.'

James frowned. 'I don't understand,' he said.

'If I don't work out every day and control my food intake, I'll put on weight. The last thing I want is to be a fat and middle-aged. I see women like that all the time. They take up a whole seat on the bus, they wear polyester trousers and have greasy hair. I couldn't bear to be like that.'

James smiled. 'You're joking, right?'

'No,' said Sophie. 'I used to be much bigger than I am now. I have to work to look like this.'

'I thought you were one of those naturally skinny girls. You don't look like you could ever get fat.'

'I'm only this small because I was in a body-building competition last weekend. Before that I was six kilos heavier.'

'To be honest,' said James. He leaned forward to look at her face. 'I don't understand why women obsess so much about their bodies. I've dated all shapes and sizes. Most men aren't that bothered. As they say, "Beauty comes from the inside".'

'It has nothing to do with being attractive to men,' said Sophie. Irritation prickled underneath her skin. 'I do it for myself. I feel better when I'm fit and strong and my clothes fit properly.'

'I can't argue with something that makes you feel better,' he said. 'But don't you miss lazy mornings in bed, bacon and eggs for breakfast and drinking cocktails on summer afternoons? That's what makes *me* feel better about myself.'

'I believe in short term sacrifices for long term rewards.'

'I've heard about that.' He laughed. 'I lean towards short-term pleasure myself. Might not be here tomorrow.'

Sophie shrugged. 'Maybe, maybe not. But you still need to plan for the future.'

'What do you have planned for the future?' James asked.

Sophie took a sip of wine. She tried to imagine what she would be doing in five years. All she saw down the long lens of the future was more of the same. Same struggle to stay thin, same shows at the Opera House, same relationship with her husband, same house in the suburbs, same, same, same. When you were young, the future was full of adventure. Who would you marry, how many kids would you have, what would your house look like, where would you work? Once all those questions had been answered, there wasn't anything left to look forward to. Sophie supposed if you had kids, you could shift your focus to them. But Michael hadn't wanted children and Sophie hadn't been ready to give up work to raise a family. She also didn't want to ruin the body she had worked so hard to create. She had taken too long to make up her mind and now it was too late.

'I'm planning to stay active and healthy into old age,' she said. It was one of her standard responses when people questioned the hours she devoted to the gym.

'Fishing,' said James. He exhaled a long, lazy sigh. 'I plan to buy a boat and fish for Black Bass.'

'Isn't Texas a long way from the ocean?'

'Rivers, lakes, reservoirs — there's plenty to choose from. I love fishing. It empties my mind.'

Sophie drank another mouthful of wine. She felt the gentle caress of alcohol start to soften the edges of her brain.

James picked up the menu. 'Do you cheat?' he asked, without looking up.

'Sorry?'

'On your diet,' he said. 'The lemon tart is exquisite. Shall I order you one?'

'No thanks,' said Sophie. 'I'm not big on sweets. But go right ahead. It doesn't bother me.'

'It's okay,' he said. 'I wanted to watch you enjoy it. I'm happy to go without.'

They sat in silence, savouring the wine, and letting the tension from the day ooze out of their bodies into the surrounding air. Whenever Sophie looked across at James, he was smiling.

'Do you have anything planned for tomorrow?' asked Sophie. Her wine glass was empty. James leaned across to refill it.

'Not beyond staying in bed late and having bacon and eggs for breakfast,' he said. 'Living in the moment.'

Sophie laughed and pulled her legs up underneath her. She let her head lean against the winged side of the armchair. Sleep made her eyes heavy. She wished someone would pull her close to their chest and breathe into her hair.

'I'd take you with me,' he said. His voice sounded strangled and strange.

She sat up, her eyes wide. 'God, I was nodding off then,' she said.

'I'd take you with me, out to Lake Amistad, away from civilisation.'

'What would we do?'

'Fish, my darling. Just fish.'

Sophie imagined lying on the deck of James' boat soaking up the summer sun. She could feel the breeze on her skin and smell the sharp odour of freshly caught fish. James cradled a fishing reel, without a shirt, his torso brown from the sun.

'We should go,' she said. She pulled her bag on to her lap. 'It's getting late.'

'Let's get another bottle,' he said.

'No.' She stood. 'I want to leave.'

CHAPTER THREE

A stabbing pain in her stomach woke Sophie at six a.m. She rushed to the en suite, grateful it was only a few steps away from the bed. She winced as the laxatives did their work.

Last night, after James had dropped her home and she had heard the door to his apartment close, Sophie had gone out. At one o'clock in the morning, the only place open was a petrol station. She could remember buying potato chips and chocolate peanuts. The thought caused a swell of nausea to rise in her throat. She didn't try to remember anything else.

She sipped on a cup of green tea while she waited for her stomach to settle. From experience she knew she needed to stay close to the bathroom for at least an hour and to keep her fluids up. She had heard about girls dying from dehydration and electrolyte imbalances from using laxatives.

Sophie didn't think she was in any danger, but it was sensible to take precautions.

She went to the toilet three more times before she felt confident enough to put on leggings and a singlet. Carrying only her iPod and her room key, she took the lift to the sixth floor. As was to be expected on a Sunday morning, the gym was deserted.

She had to stop twice during her run to go to the toilet. Her legs trembled when she stepped back onto the black belt of the treadmill. By the end of an hour, all she could manage was a slow walk. Tears of frustration mixed with the sweat on her cheeks.

Back in her apartment, Sophie sat on the balcony, letting the breeze dry the perspiration on her skin. In the street below, cars full of people on the way to church, to the markets, or to their family for Sunday lunch, drove past. A taxi pulled up outside reception and tooted its horn. She burst into tears.

The work it took to stay thin seemed too much. She wished she had been born with different genes, created slender with a flat chest and narrow hips. Or perhaps if she had been born in another historical period, where her curves would be considered beautiful rather than the result of neglect. If only she were one of those women with unflagging determination and self-control. In all other areas of her life she had no trouble being disciplined and committed — why did she struggle so much with something so simple as food?

She was forced to admit that alternating between restricting and binging was unpleasant and unhealthy. She could no longer endure the hunger, the lack of energy, the feeling of emptiness when she was dieting, or the bloated, swollen, lack of physical control in the aftermath of a binge. She no longer knew any kind of pleasure without guilt snapping at her heels. She seemed to always deserve some kind of punishment, which she administered at the gym, through the pills, by the voice of judgement in her head. She loathed herself when she was dieting — wanting to slice away at slabs of flesh to make herself thinner, and she loathed herself when she gave in — knowing she was weak, selfish and undeserving of respect.

Her entire life had become a bloody skirmish between her mind and her body — and no matter whether she was on the attack or the defence, she felt miserable. If her future promised her more of the same, she wasn't sure she could bear it. It no longer mattered if her situation was a result of misfortune or a lack of character, the time had come to end the war, to call a truce, to pack up her weapons and go home. She knew she couldn't stop binging — she had already tried and failed many times. There was only one thing left under her control — she could stop dieting.

The thought made her heart feel as though it were being squeezed by a giant hand. What would happen if she stopped chasing the goal of physical perfection? She had no idea but she needed to find out.

For a moment she imagined all her darkest fears coming true. She saw her body, lying on a couch, her creased and dimpled flesh exploding from a baggy tracksuit. She watched as the woman she might become shove chocolate and ice cream and lollies into her mouth. If that ever happened, she had an escape plan. She was an expert at losing weight. But right now, while that exaggerated projection remained only a possibility in the future, Sophie decided to stop dieting. She would no longer weigh her food, count calories or worry about the carbohydrate content of what she ate. Like an alcoholic swearing off drinking, she vowed to stop restricting her food. No more. Enough.

In the kitchen Sophie went through the cupboards. She threw away the tub of protein powder, the bottle of fat burners, the six-pack of fat-free yogurt, the creatine powder, the fish oil tablets, the packet of rice cakes and the remaining laxatives. She put the kitchen scales and measuring cups at the back of the cupboard and screwed up the sheet of paper that listed all the food she had scheduled to eat that day.

She dialled Pip's number.

'I'm a mess,' Sophie said. Her voice cracked and tears filled her eyes. 'I've been binging again and I can't do this anymore.'

'I know what that's like,' said Pip. 'For me it was wine. For weeks after comp I was plastered every night.'

'How did you stop?'

'I gave up being so hard on myself. I started listening to my body instead of beating it into submission. I stopped dieting.'

'But I'm so afraid I'll end up fat ...'

'Like me?'

'Of course not,' said Sophie. 'You're not fat. You look great. But I'm not like you. When I let myself eat whatever I want I lose control. What if I can't stop eating?'

'You will, sweetheart. I can promise you that. Now go and put on something other than gym clothes or work clothes and catch a tram to the city. Go to a bookshop and pick up a book by Shirley Reynolds called the Blessed Body.

'Isn't she some New Age weirdo?' said Sophie. 'You know I'm not into that stuff.'

'Give it a try. You might be surprised.'

'At this point I'm willing to try anything.'

'You'll be fine, sweetie. You can do this.'

'I hope so,' said Sophie. 'I don't have any other choice.'

Sophie took the small blue book out of the paper bag and sprawled out across the king-sized bed. She inhaled the vanilla baby-powder scent of fresh pages. She opened the book, cracked the spine, made it hers. On the first page she read:

You are responsible for your own life.

Every thought you believe to be true becomes your reality.

The only space where change can happen is in this moment.

Everyone suffers from self-hatred and guilt.

Everyone believes they are not good enough.

It's a lie. You can choose not to believe it.

You have the divine power of the Universe inhabiting every cell of your body.

You are perfect, whole and complete.

When you truly love yourself and forgive yourself, every breath brings you joy.

After three chapters, Sophie fell asleep. In her dream, she was walking through a forest in an ankle-length floral dress, her hair long and loose around her shoulders. Cold, furry moss tickled the bottoms of her bare feet. Just out of sight, behind the trees, she thought she heard the sound of wings.

She woke up an hour and a half later, hot and thirsty. When she took a can of Diet Coke out of the fridge, she noticed the clock on the microwave said 18:06. She dialled Michael's number, needing to hear his voice. There was no answer.

She stood outside Apartment 36 and knocked on the door. She waited for a few minutes and knocked again. The door remained closed.

A dull ache spread across her chest and settled in her throat. For the first time she paid attention to the sensation. It was familiar. At first she thought it might be disappointment, or boredom, or perhaps the beginning of anxiety. She shook her head — none of those were right. Back in her apartment the ache grew more persistent. Then she recognised it. Loneliness. She needed soothing, comforting, loving. She thought of her father, taking her swimming at the beach every afternoon when she was a child. Water would make her feel better. She grabbed her swimmers from the drawer, put them on and wrapped a towel around her hips. The door clicked closed behind her as she padded barefoot down the corridor towards the lift.

The pool was on the seventh floor, at the end of a maze of tiled passageways and glass doors. There was another person swimming lengths in the pool. His lean arms sliced through the water with barely a splash. When he reached the end of the pool, he stopped and pulled off his goggles.

'I didn't know you swam,' said James. Water dripped from his nose. Sophie sat on a bench and drew the towel around her legs.

'I didn't know you did either,' said Sophie. 'Is it warm?'

'Like a bath,' he said. 'Come in. I have a few more laps to go before I'm finished.'

He put his goggles back on and continued swimming, tumble-turning at each end. He didn't seem to be taking any notice of Sophie so it seemed safe to take off the towel and get into the water.

Although it had been years since she'd been in a pool, her body remembered the rhythm of her stroke and the timing of her breathing. After two laps she felt her mind stop. All she was aware of was the water, her breath and the beating of her heart. She felt as if she were swimming in some primordial ooze, at a time before she was born, before she formed any opinions, when everything existed in the moment, outside of time and space. The water in her veins hummed in harmony with the water surrounding her.

James sat on the edge of the pool.

'Like fishing,' he said. 'Empties my mind.'

Sophie pushed her hair out of her eyes. 'I've decided to cheat.' James raised his eyebrows. 'Well, more than that,' she said, 'I've decided to take the rest of the week off dieting. And if all goes well, maybe I won't ever go back.'

'More like a divorce than cheating.'

Sophie laughed. 'Exactly.'

'What are we doing here then? I'll meet you in the lobby in twenty minutes. I don't know if you know this, but Sunday night is burger night.'

'Not MacDonalds—'

'—God, no. Blue Train.'

Sophie realised she hadn't eaten all day. The thought

of a burger and chips made her mouth water.

'Fifteen minutes,' she said. 'I'm starving.'

Sophie woke the next morning at five a.m. even though she hadn't set the alarm. She ran her hand over her stomach, feeling a bulge underneath her hand. It seemed as though the chicken burger and chips were still sitting there from the night before. Her brain told her she should get dressed and go the gym. Work up a sweat, burn some calories and get rid of the energy her body was laying down as fat. But she couldn't do it. Instead, she made herself a cup of Earl Grey tea from the hotel supplies and put in a teaspoon of sugar. She cradled the hot mug in her hand and sat on the balcony. The tea tasted sweet and special, soothing and calming.

In the bathroom, she looked at the digital scales sitting underneath the vanity unit. She hadn't stood on them since Saturday morning, prior to her most recent binge. She contemplated weighing herself, but she didn't want to know how heavy she was getting. One day, when she was stronger, when she no longer worried about a stupid number on a machine, she would find out — but not today. She wasn't ready yet to face her disappointment.

What she couldn't escape or ignore was how she looked in the mirror. She could no longer see the definition of her abdominal muscles, or the separation of the muscles in her thighs. The bones on her chest and her hip bones seemed to be disappearing under a layer of fat. Her rings were tight on her fingers. Some of it was undoubtedly the puffiness and bloating brought about by binging but not all of it. She looked soft.   'Fat pig,' said the voice in her head, 'fat, lazy, pig.' Sophie was used to the voice so she wasn't surprised to hear it. 'Everything is perfect, whole and complete,' she said to herself. She didn't believe it.

At the computer, she searched for 'intuitive eating', a phrase she had heard mentioned in one of the online fitness forums she often visited. The principle was straightforward — eat when you're hungry, eat what you want, stop when you're full. Most people in the fitness industry scoffed at the idea, saying it was an excuse for fat people to eat junk food all day. For Sophie, someone who weighed spinach and added its calorie value to her daily allowance, it was too much of a leap. There had to be another solution.

She found Amelia Anderson's website after a few clicks. Her profile photo showed a slender blond girl with large blue eyes. In the gallery there were several before and after photos showing Amelia round and overweight in one, and lean and toned in the next. Amelia advocated 'healthy eating' without the constraints of calorie counting. Her philosophy was built around yoga and self-love through connecting with one's body. The ideas Amelia suggested appealed to Sophie. She would continue to make an effort to look after herself rather than abandon all control the intuitive eating way. She could still continue to have oats, salad, vegetables, chicken and fish as her main staples. She would shy away from packaged and healthy food and work on giving up Diet Coke. And she could still exercise.

When she realised the pool was empty, Sophie felt a pang of disappointment. It was just after six thirty a.m. so she wasn't expecting James to be there, but part of her hoped he would be. As she swam from one end of the pool to the other she thought about the night before. When they had arrived back at the hotel, James had hovered at her door, reluctant to leave. Sophie had wanted to ask him in, but she didn't trust herself. Loneliness wasn't a valid excuse for being with another man. *Being with another man*, the phrase made her laugh — even in her own thoughts she had grown uncharacteristically coy when it came to sex. It was something she never talked about. She had never discussed sex with Michael or mentioned it to Pip. It wasn't that she was prudish or embarrassed, in fact, before she had met Michael she'd had many lovers and enjoyed all kinds of sex in all different places. But a man who fucks you on the bonnet of a car isn't the kind of man a woman marries, not if she wants the marriage to last forever. Michael was intelligent, stable and more reserved than her previous boyfriends. He seemed driven by his mind rather than his body. Sophie felt sure Michael had never cheated on her. As he grew older, he didn't seem interested in sex at all.

As Sophie had grown older, the same thing had happened. She didn't miss sex with Michael and she didn't look for it elsewhere. James confused her. She enjoyed his company, she liked the attention he gave her, she felt an attraction to him but she wasn't sure what any of it meant. It wasn't as though she longed to have sex with him and was restraining herself out of loyalty to her marriage. All she wanted was to be held tenderly and to be kissed deeply. She wanted those things from Michael more than anyone else, but the thought of James' lips on hers made her heart beat faster.

CHAPTER FOUR

Sophie dragged her suitcase through the front door. 'Hi honey, I'm home,' she called. Michael appeared from the study wearing a stained grey t-shirt and black jeans. As he kissed her on the cheek, she smelt beer on his breath. She had taken the early flight, it wasn't even lunch time. She put her arms around him and hugged him. His arms remained at his sides.

He pointed at Izzy who sauntered down the hallway. 'She missed you,' he said. He went back into the study, sat at the desk and gazed at the computer monitor.

After unpacking her suitcase and putting on a load of washing, Sophie sat on the couch in the lounge room and leafed through the *Healthy Living* magazine she had bought at the airport on the way home. Izzy padded her lap before settling down to sleep.

Michael walked in carrying a DVD. He stood in front of the bookshelf with his back to her, finding the empty slot he had taken it from. 'Aren't you going to the gym today?' he asked.

'No,' said Sophie. 'I haven't been for a week.'

He turned to look at her and frowned. 'That's not like you.'

'Do you have a minute? There's something I need to talk to you about.'

'Terry and Paul said they'd come over this afternoon. Can't we do it later?'

'It won't take long.' She pointed to the armchair. 'Sit down for a second.'

Michael sat, but remained perched on the edge of the chair. He sighed. 'Well...?'

'I haven't been to the gym because my dieting and training have been out of control.' She swallowed, trying to ease the tremble in her voice. 'I don't think it's normal to be so obsessed about how I look all the time. It's hard to admit, but I might have an eating disorder.'

'You're not serious? What eating disorder?'

'Binging and purging with exercise. They call it exercise bulimia.' She didn't mention the laxatives. She was too ashamed.

'Eating disorders are for teenage girls who want attention,' he said. 'Don't be so bloody over-dramatic. There's nothing wrong with you.'

Tears welled up in Sophie's eyes. She looked down at her lap hoping he wouldn't notice.

'You're not crying, are you?' Michael's voice sounded hard and metallic. He stood up. 'Oh, for fuck's sake, Sophie.

Grow up.' He walked out.

Sophie sat weeping on the couch for several minutes before she rose to get a tissue from her handbag. Her phone flashed with a message.

I miss you already.

Sophie stared at the message for a moment, her mind refusing to interpret what the message meant or how she should respond. James' message seemed unusually intimate when, for the past week, she had kept their relationship strictly professional. Aside from dinner with the company on opening night, the only time she had seen him was at work. He still flirted with her, but she hadn't flirted back. It seemed pointless to invest so much time in something which had no future. She would never risk her marriage for something as trivial as desire.

She read the message one more time, then pressed DELETE.

The boardroom table occupied the entire length of the room. Outside a wall of glass, the grey sky dropped soft rain into the harbour, ruffling the surface of the water and smudging the outline of the yellow and green ferries that sailed past. Sophie sat at the head of the table and waited until the twelve men and women had taken their places, filled their glasses with water and opened their folders.

'Good morning, ladies and gentlemen,' she said. 'Today's scheduling meeting will cover the period from 12th-24th November. Are there any late changes before the 12th?'

George Davis, the light reflecting off his bald skull, cleared his throat. 'The Governor is attending the opening night of *Swan Lake*,' he said. 'There are no additional requirements for anyone else in the room. I'll be escorting her.'

'Thanks, George. Anything else?'

'It's nice to have you back,' said Bruce, the head of the lighting department. 'We missed you.'

'Alright,' said Sophie, smiling briefly. 'Let's start with the Opera Theatre. Page three on your print-out. Monday 12th November: Three p.m. change-over. Five p.m. class. Six-thirty *Swan Lake* performance four. Standard show crew.'

For the next hour and a half Sophie read out all of the activities that would be happening in the five venues of the Opera House. The heads of department, account managers, food and beverage operators, front of house managers and operational staff adjusted their rosters to reflect what was scheduled. The meeting was booked for two hours but she liked to get through it as quickly as possible.

Beth Turner walked back with Sophie to the Stage Management office. Sophie sat behind her desk and Beth took the chair in front.

'I've done the roster up until the 24th and I'll send it out tomorrow,' Beth said.

'Thanks,' said Sophie. 'But don't worry about sending it out. I'll look at it today and check it before it goes out.'

Beth's mouth set in a firm line. Sophie guessed she had upset her.

'It's not that I don't trust you,' said Sophie. 'I just want to get up to speed with what's going on.'

Beth nodded. Sophie thought she saw a flash of irritation cross Beth's face but it dissolved quickly into a smile.

'No worries,' said Beth. 'Makes sense.'

'Anything else I should know about?' asked Sophie.

Beth pulled a sheet of paper from a folder and laid it on the desk. 'There's this.' She pointed at the page. 'Jenna's last show.'

Sophie looked down at the document in front of her. It was a show report from the *Sydney Symphony* performance on the previous Saturday night. In the comments section Sophie read:

The area underneath the Stage Management desk is filthy. It is obvious the cleaners haven't been in for days, or if they have, they don't know how to clean properly. The dust has irritated my sinuses making it difficult to breathe. This situation is a breach of Workplace Health and Safety. I am reporting it to the nurse.

'I thought we'd gone over this,' said Sophie. 'Was I not clear about what's appropriate in a show report?'

'Perfectly clear,' said Beth. 'Jenna's not stupid. Maybe there's something else going on?'

'Have you heard from Dave? I bet he's none too pleased to have his staff criticised in public.'

'He wouldn't have seen it until this morning,' said Beth. 'There's probably something in your inbox.'

'I have a meeting with Jenna this afternoon so I'll find out what's going on. Don't worry, I'll sort it out. What else happened when I was away?'

'Nothing much. A few school concerts, the Opera-Ballet change-over and an interesting dance season in the Playhouse. The only small bit of drama happened when one of the drag queens in the Studio show fell off his heels and broke his ankle. No one is sure if he was drunk or not.'

'Worker's Comp?'

'Thankfully no. He did it on his day off at some party in Darlinghurst. They had to re-block the last show without him.'

'So business as usual,' said Sophie.

'Business as usual,' said Beth.

Sophie looked at the time on her computer. 'Let's go the Greenroom and buy lunch,' she said. 'I have six hundred emails to trawl through and I need some sustenance before I start.'

Beth looked surprised. 'Really? You didn't bring your lunch with you?'

'Not today. I'm willing to take my life into my own hands and risk the salad bar. I need you there to steer me away from the hot chips.'

'Don't worry, the hot chips are shit.'

Sophie smiled. 'Thank God.'

Sophie and the HR manager, Rebecca Gilbert, looked up as the door opened and Jenna Coppins walked in. Jenna wore red glasses and a dress that strained across her hips. Her hair was pulled back into a pony-tail which accentuated her round face.

'I can't talk much,' said Jenna, in a voice that sounded laden with the flu. 'I picked up an infection from the Concert Hall on the weekend.'

'Thank you for coming,' said Rebecca, as Jenna sat down. 'I'm not sure it's necessary for me to be here, but I'm happy to sit in if that's what you want.'

'I'm protecting my rights,' said Jenna. 'I want a witness.'

'No problem,' said Rebecca. 'But I'm just an observer. This is between you and Sophie.'

'Humph,' said Jenna, and folded her arms across her ample breasts.

'I wanted to talk to you about what you write in your show reports,' said Sophie. 'A couple of weeks ago you wrote that the children from Sandcroft Grammar School were juvenile delinquents and this weekend you suggested that the cleaning staff were incompetent. Correct?'

Jenna shrugged.

'The show report isn't the place to express your opinion,' said Sophie. 'It's your job to stick to the facts.'

'The Sandcroft kids smashed the mirror lights in two of the dressing rooms, and I've got a sinus infection because of the dust and dirt in the Concert Hall. That's the facts,' said Jenna.

'But asserting that the children are juvenile delinquents isn't. That's a value judgement.'

'I've been here eight years and no one's ever complained about my work before. If you've got a problem with the way I do things, then it's your issue not mine.'

Sophie felt the edges of her molars press together. 'Jenna,' she said. 'The reason no one's spoken to you about this before is because before the role of Head of Stage Management was created, everyone was too busy to pay much attention to what the Stage Managers were doing. I'm here to ensure we all work to the same standards — standards of professional courtesy.'

'Are you saying I'm not a professional?'

'I'm saying you need to limit your comments on the show report to detailing any problems that occurred and then demonstrating how you solved those problems or else requesting another department to provide assistance. After the Sandcroft concert all you should have said is "Facilities: Please replace the damaged mirror lights in Dressing Rooms 24 and 26".'

'I guess,' said Jenna. She looked at something on the ceiling.

'And what about the SM desk. What are the facts?'

'There is dirt and dust under the desk which is in breach of Workplace Health and Safety.'

'Still your opinion but let's work with that,' said Sophie. 'I don't think a dirty floor constitutes a Health and Safety breach, but if it did, you should have lodged a formal complaint with the OH&S committee and had them to sort it out. It doesn't belong on a report that the CEO and the Executive reads. How about simply requesting an additional cleaning service? Things get dirty, they need to be cleaned. It's not that complicated.'

'It made me sick.'

'I'm sorry about that. I can take you off your shifts until you feel better.'

'No,' said Jenna. 'I'm fine. Are we finished?'

'What are you going to do differently in future?' asked Sophie.

'I'm going to watch what I say.'

'Jenna—' said Sophie. She stopped when she felt Rebecca's hand on her forearm.

'Okay,' said Rebecca, 'It sounds like everyone is clear on how to move forward. Thanks again for coming in, Jenna.'

'Alright,' said Jenna. She left the room without saying anything else.

Sophie clenched her fists. 'Fuck,' she said.

'Sophie,' said Rebecca, 'Don't let her get to you. She's just winding you up.'

'She seems to be making it her mission in life.'

'You can't control everyone. You can offer guidance, but they won't always take it.'

'But she won't follow a simple request. It drives me crazy.'

'I find it helps to focus on the good things rather than the bad. You have a great team of girls. Think about the ones who are doing a good job rather than the one person who's causing you grief.'

Sophie smiled weakly, gathered up her notebook and pen and walked out of the meeting room with Rebecca.

Outside Sophie's office, Rebecca paused. 'We started free yoga classes on Monday nights while you were away, you should come.'

'I don't have anything to wear.'

'I've got a spare set of yoga pants you can borrow and your t-shirt's fine. See you in the Northern Foyer at five.'

'I can't leave at five,' said Sophie. 'It's the busiest time of the day.'

'No one will miss you for an hour,' said Rebecca. She smiled. 'It'll do you good.'

'Okay,' said Sophie. 'I'll give it a go.'

Sophie settled in back at her computer. Beth's head was bent over a pile of papers.

'Beth, go ahead and send out the roster tomorrow,' said Sophie. 'I don't need to look at it, I know you've done a great job. And I forgot to say thanks before for looking after everything while I was away. You're the best.'

'You're welcome,' said Beth, and smiled.

The yoga class took place in a part of the Concert Hall Northern Foyer they called the caves. Tucked in underneath the sloped arc of the sails, it was like being in an attic. The light was soft and warm and the carpet thick. Outside, the rain had stopped, and the clouds had parted revealing patches of blue sky. The sound of flute and bells spilled from a portable CD player. Yoga mats were laid out in two parallel rows. Four or five people who Sophie recognised but didn't know their names sat on the mats performing stretches. An unfamiliar woman stood at the front of the room. She was slender and petite, with short brown hair. She reminded Sophie of a pixie.

'I'm Anisha,' said the woman at the front of the room. 'Come in and grab a mat. We'll get started in a minute.'

Soon every mat was full but the room remained hushed, like inside a cathedral.

'Let's start with child's pose, Balasana.'

It didn't take long for Sophie to realise that muscle strength and cardio fitness counted for nothing in yoga. Though the poses looked simple when Anisha did them, Sophie found it difficult to get her limbs into the right position. And staying still was the hardest part of all. Sophie kept thinking she was wasting her time. She wasn't working hard enough to burn calories and every time she stopped to focus on her breath she thought of all the things she could be doing instead. She didn't understand the point of it.

'Let your thoughts go and concentrate on your body,' said Anisha. 'Feel the mat beneath your feet, the lengthening of your hip, your fingers pressing together, the warmth in your chest.'

Sophie found it strange to be thinking about her body, a body that always seem to want something other than what was good for it. Over the years she had mastered the art of ignoring the pain in her muscles, the growling in her stomach. She suspected her body had long ago run out of things to say.

She looked around at the people beside her. Men and women alike appeared to be able to bend their bodies into positions she didn't think possible. Heads on knees, hands to feet, all without any apparent effort. None of them were in particularly good shape, but it didn't seem to matter.

'Keep pushing down into the earth with your feet, feel the energy ground you, stabilise you. Imagine the roots of a tree growing out through your feet into rich warm soil.'

After about twenty-five minutes, Sophie realised that striving to be better than anyone else was futile and that escaping early was not an option. When she was sure no one was paying her any attention she decided to take it easy for the rest of the class. She didn't look at anyone else, she just listened to Anisha's voice and followed her commands. She breathed, she felt the earth, and for a moment she thought she might have felt warmth in her chest. Earlier than Sophie expected, Anisha instructed everyone to lie down on their backs. Savasana. Corpse pose.

Lying on the floor doing nothing was a strange experience. Sophie felt disconnected from herself, as though she were floating in the ocean or in the middle of the sky. When she breathed she could almost taste the air in the back of her throat — golden, sweet, liquid. The voice in her head seemed to have stopped talking except for the words —

perfect, whole, complete. This time she believed it. And when she did, she was flooded with an overwhelming sense of joy.

CHAPTER FIVE

Stage managing performances kept Sophie alive, so she was careful to spend some of her time away from the office and on the stage. She was in the Concert Hall running rehearsal for a one night performance with Cristophe Velis, the Greek god of pop music.

Sophie stood at the front of the stage and faced the twelve-piece band.

'Ladies and Gentlemen, we're going to run through the lighting cues to make sure we have your sconces plotted into every cue so you can see your music stands. If you could put down your instruments for a few minutes, we'll get this done as quickly as possible.'

Every player put their instruments in their laps or on the floor and looked at her expectantly. These musicians were so different from the orchestral players who never paid attention to anything other than the newspaper or novel they kept hidden under their music.

'Freddy, we're going to flash through the cues to check we've got everyone covered,' she said over her headset. 'Let's start with pre-show and take it from there. Give me a sec to get back to prompt corner.'

Sophie looked at the changes of lighting states on the monitor. The Concert Hall had a solid wall between her and the stage. Someone had installed a window in the wall, but it was covered with a blind to prevent her reading lamp leaking through.

When the cues were complete, Sophie went back on stage. 'I'd like to run the first number in real time with the music so you know what to expect.' She gestured to an older man in a black polo shirt standing next to her. 'This is Bruce, the head of lighting. He's kindly offered to stand in for Cristophe Velis.' The band gave him a light round of applause. 'Remember, you're already pre-set on stage when the audience come in. Your cue to begin is once I've finished the announcement and the house lights go out. Okay everyone, please standby.'

Sophie again disappeared to the side of stage.

'House lights to half — GO.' She switched off her show loop microphone and turned on the PA microphone.

'Good evening Ladies and Gentleman and welcome to this evening's performance of Cristophe Velis in Concert. May I remind you that the use of photographic equipment and recording devices is strictly prohibited. May I also remind you to please switch off your mobile phones. Thank you.'

She switched microphones.

'House Lights out and LXQ 1 — GO.'

She heard the band start to play the first few chords of the opening sequence and smiled. The overture lasted three minutes and then transitioned into the introduction to the first song.

'Dome one and two, please standby to pick up Mr Velis as he enters stage left on your visual.' She put her hand over her mic. 'On you go, Bruce,' she said. 'Domes, he's on his way.'

As Sophie switched off her microphone she felt someone behind her. She turned to see Cristophe Velis standing in the wings.

'Have I been replaced?' he asked. His smile flashed white in the darkness.

'Only for this afternoon,' said Sophie. 'Bruce can't sing very well so we'll need you tonight.' Cristophe Velis laughed. 'I'm Sophie,' she said. He took her outstretched hand and lifted it to his lips. His kiss felt hot against her skin. 'Pleased to meet you, Sophie.'

'Do you want to go on, or are you happy to watch?' she asked. He hadn't released her hand.

'As much as it pains me to drag myself away from you,' he said, his finger stroking the base of her thumb, 'I should warm up the vocal cords.'

Sophie felt a blush warm her cheeks. She disengaged her hand.

'But don't say anything to Bruce,' he said, 'I want it to be a surprise.'

Sophie moved from the desk to the place where a large door opened onto the stage. She wanted to see Bruce's reaction.

The band noticed Cristophe Velis first and nodded
their head to him in greeting. Bruce stood at the front of the
stage and looked up at a truss supporting the lights
positioned over the auditorium. When Cristophe Velis put
his hand on Bruce's back, Bruce jumped, turned around and
then laughed when he recognised the star. He shook
Cristophe Velis' hand and passed him the microphone.

'I guess we're sound checking as well now,' said
Sophie. 'Cristophe Velis wants to sing.'

That evening, the Concert Hall was sold out. The
audience consisted of mostly women in their thirties and
forties who had been mesmerised by Cristophe Velis'
mischievous personality and his ability to make it seem as
though he were singing directly to them about how much he
wanted them.

At ten minutes to eight, everyone was held in the
twilight between finishing their pre-show preparations and
waiting for the show to start. Sophie ran over the cue sheet
on her desk, making sure she knew where every cue was
positioned. The operators all took responsibility for what to
do, they just needed Sophie to tell them when.

From the auditorium Sophie heard the sound of
excited voices, calls of greeting and shrieks of laughter.

'Sounds like they're a lively bunch.' Cristophe Velis
stood framed by blue light at the entrance to the wings. He
wore a slim-fitting grey suit with a mandarin collar. His
white shirt was also collarless. His dark wavy hair swooped
down over one eyebrow.

Sophie nodded. 'You have lots of fans.'

Cristophe Velis made his way towards Sophie. He

stood close enough so she could smell his aftershave. His skin was the shade of toast, and unblemished. He had shaved so closely that Sophie was unable to detect a trace of stubble on his chin. Young, still in his twenties. Still a child.

'So tell me about you?' asked Cristophe Velis. 'How are you doing?'

'I'm fine.' Sophie smiled.

'No, I'm serious,' he said. 'Tell me how things are going. I want to know.'

It was the first time someone had wanted to know about her in a long time. How was she doing? Not so great. Now that she had given up devoting all her energy to planning her diet and training her body, large gaps of space had opened up in her life. She didn't know how to fill them. She didn't fit in with her fitness friends online, and she couldn't bother Pip all the time. Michael didn't seem to be interested in what Sophie was doing, but that wasn't new, she just noticed it more. She felt restless, lost, drifting along without any idea where she was going.

'Have you read the Narnia book *The Magician's Nephew*?' she asked.

'Yes. I love CS Lewis.'

'In the book, Polly and Digory put on magic rings which take them to a sleepy wooded place which turns out not to be their destination, but a world between worlds. That's where I am right now. I've left one place and I'm on my way somewhere else, but at the moment, I'm stuck in the world between worlds, in limbo.'

'I understand what you mean,' said Cristophe Velis. 'I've been there myself.' He touched her arm. 'You describe it so beautifully. You'd better be careful, I might steal the idea and write a song.'

'Go right ahead,' said Sophie. 'But you might have to pay off CS Lewis' estate.'

A light flashed on the desk to indicate the phone was ringing. 'Prompt Corner,' said Sophie.

'It's Peter, from Front of House,' said the voice on the phone. 'Everyone's in. You're right to go.'

'Thanks Peter. I'll ring the bells three minutes before the end so you know when they're coming out.'

'Cheers,' said Peter.

Sophie turned to Cristophe Velis who was pacing the floor and humming quietly to himself. 'Here we go,' she said. 'Have a good show.'

Cristophe Velis stood still, stopped humming and listened to Sophie call the opening sequence. Once the band had started playing, he put his arm around her shoulder.

'Ouch, that trumpet player is flat. He needs to blow harder.' Cristophe Velis' eyes danced as he laughed.

'That's not your band?'

'No I just rent one in each city. Most of what you hear is pre-recorded on *ProTools*, but don't tell anyone.'

Sophie wrestled with the urge to tell Cristophe Velis he should be getting ready to go onstage but she decided he knew his own show and would do things in his own time, no matter what she said.

He leaned down and kissed Sophie on the lips, catching her by surprise. The kiss ended as quickly as it began, the kind of kiss you give an intimate friend or an old lover you no longer sleep with but still adore. Sophie's face arranged itself into an expression of shock.

'You'll find your way home soon, I promise,' he

whispered in her ear. Sophie felt the drop in air temperature on her neck as he moved to the side of stage. The music changed.

'Dome one and two, please standby to pick up Mr Velis as he enters stage left on your visual,' she said. Cristophe Velis gave Sophie a small wave and walked out into the light. 'He's on his way.'

Cristophe Velis sang flawlessly, told gentle jokes, and made every woman in the audience fall in love with him. Two hours later he came off stage, breathing heavily, his eyes wild. The audience clapped and yelled and banged the soles of their shoes on the polished timber floorboards. He shrugged off his jacket revealing a shirt soaked through with perspiration and placed the discarded garment into Sophie's outstretched hand. He slipped his arm around her waist, pulled her to him and kissed her for a full ten seconds. Sophie stiffened at first and then relaxed into his chest. His tongue slipped gently into her mouth just before he pulled away. He grinned and disappeared back onto the stage for his encore.

Sophie forgot to warn the Dome operators he was coming back on stage. Fortunately, they were expecting him and picked him up. Her pulse prickled through her lips against her fingertips.

When Cristophe Velis came off stage at the end of the concert, he took the jacket Sophie had put over the back of the chair and went to his dressing room without pausing to say anything. The show was over, the magic had gone, waiting to be conjured up in another theatre, in another city, on another night. It was the transience of performance, moments charged with meaning and emotion which disappeared once the curtain fell and the house lights came up. It was what Sophie both loved and hated about her job. So much beauty and feeling disappeared like wisps of fog evaporating underneath the heat of the morning sun.

Sophie put her backpack down in the dining room and kicked off her shoes. She was hungry and hadn't eaten much for dinner. Her appetite always seemed to disappear before a show. She opened the fridge and searched for something to eat. A plastic container of what looked like curry hadn't been there when she had left this morning. Michael must have had Indian for dinner.

'What kind of curry did you get?' she called.

'Beef vindaloo,' Michael shouted from the study. 'Have it if you want.'

'No thanks, too spicy.'

She pulled out a loaf of bread which the label proclaimed was wheat-free and yeast-free. It tasted like cardboard but it was healthy.

Michael walked into the kitchen while she was waiting for the toaster to finish cooking the bread. 'You look pleased with yourself,' he said. He took a long-neck bottle of VB from the fridge.

'I need you to kiss me,' said Sophie.

Michael squinted at her. 'Don't be weird,' he said. He took the lid off the beer with the bottle opener.

'Can you just kiss me?'

'Do I have to?' said her husband. The toaster beeped and the bread popped up.

'Tonight at work, Cristophe Velis kissed me on the lips at the end of the show. I need you to kiss me to cancel it out.'

'Why would he kiss *you* when he could get any woman he wanted? He's not desperate, surely?' Michael headed back towards the study.

'So I guess that's a no, then,' she said to his retreating back. She put the toast on a side plate, buttered it and spread a thick coating of Vegemite on top.

She was putting her empty plate in the dishwasher when Michael called out from the study. 'Is that true?' he said, 'Did that slimy bastard Velis really kiss you?'

Sophie went in to him. 'Yes,' she said. 'It was only a peck though, nothing to worry about.'

Michael's eyes didn't leave his computer screen. 'I've arranged a gaming session with a guy in Dusseldorf in an hour. Don't wait up for me.'

'You can't go to work tomorrow without any sleep,' she said.

He looked at her with cold eyes. 'Stop criticising me. I don't need your help.'

It was almost three a.m. before Sophie went to sleep. When she woke up it was after nine and Michael had already left for work. She wasn't needed at the Opera House until lunchtime so she padded around the house in a t-shirt and shorts, not knowing what to do with herself. On the kitchen bench, she counted twelve empty long-neck bottles of beer. Not only was Michael at work without any sleep he was probably still drunk as well.

It was a warm November morning, hot enough to suggest that it might reach over thirty degrees by the afternoon. The North Sydney pool was quiet, the early morning exercisers having gone to work and the frazzled mothers not yet arrived. Sophie swam over to the slow lane and chose breaststroke to glide through the water.

Sophie's thoughts were stuck on Michael. Ever since she had returned from Melbourne, he had seemed more angry and depressed than normal. Never one to be optimistic, he appeared to be getting worse. He found fault in everything she did. The bathroom wasn't clean enough, the dishwasher wasn't loaded properly, the bottles were stacked the wrong way in the recycling tub. His offhand comments were what hurt the most. You're getting old, you're no longer attractive, you let people take advantage of you, you're only interested in yourself, you're hurtful and unkind. Perhaps he was right. Sophie had found herself judging Michael's decisions. He hated his job in the bookshop but he didn't try to find anything else. He spent all his money on DVDs and gaming subscriptions. He rarely left the house on the weekends. She should try to keep her opinions to herself, leave him alone. It was easier than upsetting him.

She stopped at the shallow end to catch her breath. Puddles of water turned the concrete from white to grey. When she thought about leaving Michael and being on her own, a space opened up in her chest and began to ache. She didn't want to give up on her marriage when it got tough. She wasn't a quitter or a failure. It was just a stage they were going through. She had lost sight of herself as it was, she didn't want to be alone without knowing who she was. Finding herself in the world between worlds, she needed someone familiar. Michael was that person. He had watched her travel around the world, build a darkroom in the laundry, paint herself orange and parade in a bikini, without suggesting she settle down. They had a partnership, equal independence, freedom. Sophie didn't want to lose him. She loved him for never asking her why she did the things she did.

Sophie swam a few more lengths before she got out of the pool and lay in the sun. On the way home, she heard a kookaburra singing his laughing song. The ache in her chest remained.

CHAPTER SIX

'**Happy birthday to** you,' sang Beth and Jenna, as they walked into the office holding a box containing six iced cupcakes. Sophie laughed at their off tune harmonies. Beth handed her a card in a blue envelope. 'Everyone signed it,' she said.

Sophie opened the card, which had a bemused-looking cat in a party hat on the front, and read the messages inside. She pinned it on the noticeboard behind her desk.

'Gluten-free carrot cake make with honey,' said Jenna, pointing at the cupcakes. 'Beth said they had to be healthy.'

'Did *you* make these?' asked Sophie.

Jenna pushed her red glasses up her nose. 'Yes. My sister's got celiac disease.'

Sophie bit into a cupcake. 'Oh my God,' she said. The tartness of lemon icing and the sweetness of honey collided on her tongue. 'So, so good.'

'Happy birthday,' called George, and waved as he walked past the door. Sophie waved back.

Beth and Jenna took a cupcake each. 'Thank you, ladies,' she said, 'I feel very special.'

Sophie's mobile phone beeped with a message.

Have a wonderful birthday. Wish I was there. x

Sophie hadn't heard from James since the day she had arrived home from Melbourne two months ago. She had thought he'd forgotten about her. She didn't know how he knew it was her birthday. She typed her response, her thumbs gliding over the small keyboard on her Blackberry.

Thanks. I wish you were here.

She pushed send and then stared at the message she had just sent. Why had she written that she wished he were here? Never mind, she couldn't do anything about it now.

'Is there a birthday girl in here?' a familiar voice called. Sophie looked up to see Pip standing in the doorway, a leather overnight bag slung over her shoulder.

'No way,' said Sophie. She rushed to her friend to give her a hug. 'I didn't know you were coming. You didn't say.'

'I arranged it all with Michael in secret. We wanted to surprise you.' Pip dropped her bag on the floor. 'Happy birthday, gorgeous.'

'Thanks for the wonderful surprise. How long are you here for?'

'I fly back Monday morning, so I'm all yours for the weekend.'

'Fantastic,' said Sophie. 'Pip, this is Jenna Coppins

and Beth Turner and those on my desk are cupcakes. Have one.'

Pip kissed both women on the cheek and picked up a cupcake. 'Looks like I got here at exactly the right time.'

Beth smiled at Sophie. 'Go on,' said Beth. 'Take the afternoon off. I've got it covered.'

Sophie only hesitated for a minute. She logged off the computer and picked up her handbag. 'Call me on the mobile if you need me, girls. Have a great weekend.'

'Bye,' called Pip, as she followed Sophie out the door.

The ferry trip from Circular Quay to Milsons Point took ten minutes. Sophie and Pip sat on a wooden bench outside in the sun and watched the side of the ferry slice through the water, creating swirls of white foam. The ferry was almost empty. In a week or two it would be packed full of tourists and holidaying locals taking a break over summer.

'You look great,' said Pip, squeezing Sophie's hand.

Sophie frowned. 'Do you think? I grew out of my comp jeans a couple of weeks ago and now these size tens are feeling tight. I hope I don't keep getting fatter and fatter.'

'It's not like you're pigging out on pies and chocolate every day. You'll be fine.'

'My food's okay but I'm not doing nearly as much exercise as before. Swimming three mornings a week and yoga on Monday nights. It's not enough.'

'Don't worry about it,' said Pip. 'To be honest, you looked too skinny and fragile at your comp weight. You look more beautiful now than you did then.'

'You're just saying that because it's my birthday.' Sophie grinned.

'I mean it, Soph. You're gorgeous.'

They walked up the hill to Sophie and Michael's house, grateful for the shade of the trees overhanging the footpath. Sophie showed Pip to the spare room at the end of the hallway. Michael had put fresh sheets on the bed and a folded towel on top of the bedspread.

Pip pulled a large parcel from her bag. The present was wrapped in orange paper with silver stars. 'Open it,' she said.

Sophie found a purple yoga mat inside the parcel.

'I shouldn't have folded it,' said Pip, 'but it was the only way to get it in my bag.'

'I love it,' said Sophie. She pressed the soft fabric to her cheek.

'Drape it over a chair — the creases will fall out in no time.' Pip handed her a square case. 'And this goes with it. It's a DVD full of yoga classes.'

'How did you know?' asked Sophie.

'Michael told me.'

'Thank you for coming down and thank you for the presents. Now, we should go get a drink.'

Sophie and Pip walked a block and a half to a small Italian cafe. They sat outside underneath the awning and watched people walking up and down the street. A woman tied her small dog to a parking meter and sat down at a table nearby. Her hair was almost pure white and braided into a long plait that followed the line of her backbone. Black Gucci sunglasses sat on top of her head.

'How did you do it?' asked Sophie. She sipped on a tall glass of vodka, lime and soda. 'How did you avoid regaining all the weight you lost when you competed?'

'I didn't,' said Pip. 'All the weight came back as well as some extra. Anyone who tells you you can maintain twelve percent body fat is either lying or delusional.'

'How did you deal with it?'

'You mean aside from the drinking?' Pip laughed. 'I woke up one morning with a shocking hangover and realised I couldn't keep doing what I was doing. I had all sorts of problems — no period, constipation, always cold, no sex drive, muscle pain, no energy — and I was always, always ravenously hungry. I had to eat or I would have gone mad. Once I got back to what was a normal weight for me, all that shit went away. I'd rather be healthy and happy than skinny.'

'Did you feel a bit... I don't know... like you didn't fit in anymore?'

'I've never been one of the fitness crowd. They're all too intense for me. I see them at the gym in their *Lorna Jane* sports bras and fake breasts looking down their noses at me wearing my dad's t-shirt and runners full of holes. I don't care. Life's too short to get hung up on all that shit.'

Sophie heard the old lady with the braided hair order apple pie and ice cream. The waiter paused at their table.

'Can I get you ladies another drink?' he asked.

'No, thank you,' said Sophie. 'We're fine for now.'

'Work, Nathan, the dogs, training, mum and dad — they all keep me busy,' said Pip, after the waiter had gone. 'I just get on with it.'

Sophie heard her phone vibrate in her bag. 'Sorry, hon. Might be work.'

The name James Parkin flashed up on her screen.

'Mr Parkin, as I live and breathe,' said Sophie.

'What are you doing,' said James, 'in the middle of an

Australian summer?'

'Pip and I are sitting in the sun drinking vodka, lime and soda.'

'Told you I wished I was there.'

Sophie laughed.

'I love the sound of your laugh.' said James. 'It's good to hear your voice.'

'It's good to talk to you too.' Sophie grimaced. She wished she could think of something more interesting to say.

'I won't keep you from your drink,' he said. 'I just wanted to wish you a happy birthday... again.'

'Thanks, James.'

'Bye, my darling,' he said and hung up.

Pip raised an eyebrow at Sophie. Sophie drank the last of her vodka, the straw making a sucking noise on the ice. 'Would you like another?' she asked, nodding her head toward Pip's almost empty glass.

'Not so fast, young lady,' said Pip. 'James?'

Sophie giggled, then tried to look serious but couldn't stop smiling.

'Look at you,' said Pip. 'It's been a long time since I've seen you look... I don't know... happy. Come on, spill.'

'It's nothing,' said Sophie. 'He was the production manager in Melbourne. He's nice. I'm married. The end.'

'I don't think so,' said Pip. 'Are you having an affair?'

'Yes, Pip. He's in Texas and I'm in Sydney and we meet in Hawaii every second Tuesday for an afternoon shag.'

The waiter passing their table appeared to have overheard Sophie's last couple of words because he stopped and grinned at her. She smiled back and held up her empty glass.

Pip leaned across the table and grabbed Sophie's hands. 'Wouldn't it be amazing if you did?'

'My husband might not think so.'

'Don't tell him,' said Pip. 'Seriously though, what's this James like?'

'I told you, he's nice. But nothing's going on I promise.'

'What does he look like?'

Sophie laughed. 'Enough already. Can we talk about something else?'

'If you insist,' said Pip.

The waiter delivered two fresh drinks to the table and collected the empty glasses. He seemed unable to take his eyes of Sophie.

'You must be doing something right,' said Pip. 'That waiter looked like he wanted to eat you.'

'Oh, Pip,' said Sophie, 'you make me laugh. You're exactly what I needed.' She raised her glass. 'Here's to us.'

'To us.'

The long wooden table was lit with tall cathedral candles in glass vases. Fairy lights were draped across the window frames. The room smelled of lemongrass and ginger. Sophie and Pip were engrossed in the menu when Michael walked in.

'Good evening, ladies,' he said. 'You both look gorgeous.' He kissed Pip on the cheek and sat down next to Sophie. When he kissed his wife on the lips, he tasted of coffee and cigarettes.

'I hear you're responsible for keeping Pip's visit from me,' said Sophie.

Michael winked at Pip. 'It was our little secret,' he said. He looked around for the waitress and signalled her over.

'Can I get a schooner of beer and two red wines, please?' He draped his arm over the back of his wife's chair and leaned back. With his free hand, he pulled a small gift bag from his pocket. 'For you,' he said. 'Happy birthday.'

Inside the bag, inside the tissue paper, Sophie discovered a slim silver bracelet. He took the gift from her and slipped it over her hand.

'Thank you,' said Sophie. 'It's lovely.'

Later, after the trio had eaten their fill of tasty Thai cuisine, Sophie and Pip sat together on the bed in the guest room. They wore their pyjamas, their faces shining after being scrubbed free of makeup.

'Michael's such a sweetie,' said Pip. 'You're lucky to have him.'

Sophie nodded. The version of Michael in the restaurant was indeed sweet, but he wasn't the man she lived with every day. Michael's ability to turn on the charm in public was the main reason she kept her unhappiness to herself. Everyone who knew him would never believe he could be difficult, that he never touched her, that he was so easily upset. It occurred to her that if he could be pleasant with everyone else, then she must be the problem. She knew she possessed many faults and flaws. After all these years, she shouldn't be surprised if his patience had run out.

'It was a lovely evening,' said Sophie. She touched the silver bracelet on her wrist. 'It's been a great day. The best birthday ever.'

'I'm glad,' said Pip. 'You deserve it.'

'Do you have everything you need?'

'I think so.' Pip pulled back the covers and slid into the bed. 'Soph, you're doing great. You're only a couple months out from comp and you're eating healthy and doing exercise you enjoy. You haven't binged in all that time. That's a huge accomplishment. You've got this. You should be proud.'

'Really?' said Sophie. 'Then why have I been feeling so out of sorts?'

'Maybe it's your hormones, have you thought of that?'

'Perhaps you're right.' Sophie leaned down to kiss her friend on the forehead. 'Goodnight, hon, I love you.'

'Goodnight,' said Pip. 'I love you too.'

CHAPTER SEVEN

Sophie waved as the taxi taking Pip to the airport pulled away from the curb. She closed the front door and sighed a contented sigh. She had spent the last two days with Pip taking walks along the Harbour foreshore, getting massages, shopping for clothes and eating delicious food. Michael had been in a great mood all weekend and had cooked garlic prawns and his special fried rice on Sunday night. The lost feeling that had dogged her for the last few months seemed to have faded. She felt lucky to have a nice home, a loving husband, a best friend and a great job. She still didn't like what she saw in the mirror, but perhaps she never would. She had heard that competing ruins the way you see yourself for the rest of your life because you're always comparing yourself to your lowest ever weight. If that was the worse problem she had to live with, then things would be okay.

In the bathroom, she looked down at the scales which were covered in a film of dust. She hadn't yet been brave enough to stand on them. Was today the day? She stood underneath the shower and washed her hair while she considered her decision. She had drunk a cup of tea but hadn't eaten anything. The meal the night before was home cooked and light so she shouldn't be holding any water. The veins on her hands and feet were visible and her rings moved around her fingers. She had been doing everything right for the past eight weeks. No refined sugar, no wheat, no highly processed junk food. Although she might have overdone it occasionally on the macadamia nuts, or the dates, or the frozen yogurt and carob buds, she hadn't binged. Without writing down the calorie values of her food, she calculated in her head that she was eating around two thousand a day. Some of her clothes fitted and some of them didn't — probably, she assumed, because her shape had changed since she had given up lifting heavy weights. She estimated that she should have only gained a few kilos, perhaps a bit more if she took the cup of tea into account.

Naked and shivering, Sophie stood on the scales. She closed her eyes, exhaled and then looked down. The black display panel flashed up a strange and startling number. Sophie couldn't believe it. The scales must be malfunctioning from lack of use. She turned them off, walked around the bathroom for a minute and then switched them back on. This time she stepped on with purpose, as if daring the machine to do its worst.

Ten kilos. Ten.

Ten kilos more than the morning of competition day. That was the six she had lost before the show plus four more.

She kicked the scales back under the vanity and burst into tears. All her efforts had been for nothing. She might as well have eaten pies and chocolate and not moved off the couch. She looked in the mirror, trying to see what she had missed. Her breasts, her thighs and her backside were fuller, her stomach had a gentle curve, but she couldn't identify where all the fat had gone. She must be delusional. She had wanted so badly to look normal that she had grown heavy and ugly without even noticing. 'Fat pig,' said the voice in her head. 'Fat pig,' she said, out loud.

Sophie completed the Monday morning scheduling meeting in seventy minutes, barely looking up from the page. If her colleagues were surprised by her abruptness, none of them took the time to ask her what was wrong. When she walked back into her office, Jenna was sitting in front of the computer with a large square Tupperware container at her elbow.

'What's that?' asked Sophie.

'Lunch,' said Jenna. 'I've signed up for Weight Watchers. I made a salad.'

Sophie pressed her arms against the sides of her body, feeling the spongy softness of the fat on her hips yield to the pressure from her elbows.

'Weight Watchers is shit,' said Sophie. Jenna seemed surprised and then angry. The fragile truce they had maintained for the past few weeks shattered. Sophie pulled down the show report folder and scanned the documents from the weekend. Jenna stopped typing and waited, her face contracting into a scowl.

'There's nothing there,' said Jenna. The report was for

a client who Jenna had worked for every year for the past eight years. Jenna had never said anything critical about the company. The report was clean.

Sophie closed the folder and put it back on the bookshelf. She picked up her handbag. 'I'm going for lunch,' she said. 'Off site.'

On her walk to Circular Quay, Sophie couldn't decide what to eat. Part of her wanted to restrict, to cut out all carbohydrates and only have protein. The other part of her wanted to devour all the greasy junk food she could get her hands on. She stood outside MacDonald's waiting for some kind of sign. All she saw were teenage boys with spotty faces leaving the store carrying brown paper bags. She walked in and ordered two cheese burgers, fries and a Diet Coke. She waited until she was sitting on a bench, close to the water before she took a mouthful of the first burger. The meat was dry and the cheese like plastic. She threw the burgers in the bin. The fries were cold but she ate them anyway.

Back in the office, Jenna had disappeared and Beth was pinning up fresh copies of the roster. She looked at Sophie as she threw her bag in the corner.

'Bad day?' asked Beth.

'I've had better,' said Sophie.

'Anything I can do?'

'I don't think so.'

Beth moved to the chair in front of Sophie's desk. 'This may not be the right time to ask,' Beth said, 'but I was wondering if you still took photos.'

'I suppose so,' said Sophie. 'I still have all the gear but it's been a while.'

'I was thinking it would be nice to have some photos

of Max and me now he's getting older. You know, send them to the family for Christmas. But I don't want any of those hideous portraits with the suede backgrounds. I was imagining something outside in the park.' Beth smiled. 'I would pay you of course, that's if you're interested.'

Sophie had only met Max a couple of times when Beth had bought him in for the kids' shows. He was a wiry nine-year-old with orange freckles and spiked hair. He called Sophie 'Miss Walker,' and loved Harry Potter. Sophie could think of worse ways to spend her time than hanging out in the park with him and his mother.

'I'd love to,' said Sophie. 'But you don't need to pay me. I'm out of practice so they'll probably be crap.'

'Are you sure? I'm happy to pay.'

'If by some miracle I come up with a masterpiece, you can let me use it to advertise my talents one day in the future. Let's just call it a workshop.'

'Could we do it tomorrow night after work if we sneak off early? It stays light until eight. At the park near my place?'

'Give me the details and I'll be there.' Sophie felt a small buzz of excitement at the base of her skull. She would have to pull her DSLR out of the cupboard tonight, clean the lenses and charge the batteries.

The phone on Sophie's desk rang. Beth smiled and gave Sophie a thumbs up before going back to her computer.

'I'm working on next year's schedule,' said Kim Chen, on the phone, 'and I wanted to check your availability.'

A sliver of light shone through the blackness of the day. Kim Chen wanted to work with Sophie again. She must have done a good job.

'We have a grant to take *Fault Lines* to the States,' he said. 'Would you be interested?'

'Of course,' said Sophie. 'I'd love to come.'

'We'll probably need you for a whole month — ten days of rehearsals, travel time and two weeks in South Carolina. Originally we thought about February, but that's when James is getting married, so we've decided on April.'

Sophie's heart seemed to stop beating and she felt as though she couldn't get enough air into her lungs. Her breath became short and shallow, like she had just finished sprinting. James married. Was this something new or had James been engaged from the moment she had first met him? He had lied to her, or at least, not told her everything. She wanted to call him and ask for an explanation. But she had no right to care. She wasn't any part of his life, she couldn't be. He didn't have to explain himself to her.

'I'm sorry, Kim Chen, did you say April?'

'April, yes.'

'I'll need to check with my boss but I don't see a problem. Send through the contract and I'll work things out this end.'

'We're also planning to create a new piece in the second half of next year. It would be great if you could work with us from the very beginning. Nothing concrete yet but I'll let you know.'

'I'd love that.'

'You're the best Stage Manager I've ever worked with,' said Kim Chen. 'From now on I have to have you on all my shows.'

'Thank you. Let's talk soon.'

Sophie put down the handset and looked across at

Beth. 'Do you have any plans for April next year?' asked Sophie.

Beth shook her head.

'You do now,' said Sophie. 'You're the acting Head of Stage Management for a month.'

'Cool,' said Beth. 'Where are you going?'

'South Carolina. I've never been to the States.'

'That's one way to brighten up a bad day,' said Beth.

'You're not wrong,' said Sophie. Except it still was a bad day. James was getting married and without any reason she could articulate, Sophie felt hurt. The kind of hurt that reaches into your stomach, pulls your intestines out onto the floor and then stomps on them. The bleeding, dying kind of hurt. Sophie wanted to cry but she forced herself not too. She had been crying altogether too much recently. It would have to stop.

That night, while Sophie picked at her chicken salad and Michael ate pizza in front of the television, she told him about the job in the States.

'Kim Chen wants me on all his shows from now on,' she said. 'He said I'm the best SM he's ever worked with.'

'He probably only said that because he's been through every other stage manager and no one wants to put up with him,' he said. 'You probably let him get away with murder so of course he wants you around.'

Sophie looked at her husband, barely able to believe what she was hearing. 'Is that what you think, seriously?' she said, her voice cracking. She felt the tremble start in the back of her throat and spread to her whole body.

'You let people take advantage of you, it's always

been your problem. You're too accommodating, especially to dickheads.'

'I don't—'

'—Funny how you're so nice to everyone else and such a bitch to me.'

'What do you mean—'

'—Save it for your theatre buddies.' Michael sighed. 'I'm too fucking tired for this tonight. I'll see you later.' He went to the fridge, collected a beer, walked to the study and slammed the door.

Sophie sat on the couch, stunned and still trembling. It seemed as though Michael hated her. A stabbing pain cut through her ribs. She looked at the pizza box. There were three pieces left. She was full but she thought about eating more. First, she would succumb to the sensory pleasure of crust, salty bacon, fatty cheese and rich tomato sauce, her thoughts silenced by the pleasure. Once the food was gone, the voice in her head would berate her for being so weak and undisciplined, while at the same time she would be distracted by trying to find a way to relieve her physical discomfort. She would need to think about how to get rid of the calories she had just consumed, either by taking laxatives, doing extra exercise in the morning, or both. What was clear was that if she started a binge, she wouldn't have to think about how fat she was, about James getting married, or about Michael's disgust.

But she couldn't do it.

The one thing she could rely on to take the edge off her pain was gone. She couldn't binge. How many more things would she have to lose before the losses stopped?

Her phone rang. It was Pip. She must have felt

Sophie's need to talk to someone.

'I rang to say thank you for the weekend,' said Pip. 'It was amazing.'

'You're more than welcome. It was great seeing you.'

'And I've got some news. You'll never guess what I've decided to do next year.'

'You and Nathan are getting married?' said Sophie.

'Not likely.' Pip laughed. 'I've decided to compete again. I'm going to do *Fitness Mania* in March and I want you there to glue my bikini to my arse.'

'Of course,' said Sophie.

'This is going to be the last time. We're going to try for a baby once I'm done.'

'Oh, sweetheart. That's wonderful news. Why wait though, couldn't you get pregnant now?'

'Just one last shot, Soph, then it'll be out of my system. I know you understand.'

'Congratulations. Sounds like next year will be huge.'

'I know.' Pip giggled. 'Anyway, how are things?'

Sophie looked down at her thighs, at the empty pizza box and at the closed door of the study. 'Perfect,' she said. 'Things couldn't be more perfect.'

'Great,' said Pip. 'Gotta go, Nathan can't find the remote. Bye.'

The phone beeped the disconnect tone. She switched it off and put it on the coffee table. She thought she might cry but her eyes remained dry. She felt sick and tired and disappointed. The last two months she had tried so hard to turn her life around and instead of getting better, everything had got worse. She was beaten, bruised and bleeding and had no idea what to do next.

CHAPTER EIGHT

When Sophie woke the next morning, Michael's side of the bed hadn't been slept in. In the lounge room there was a blanket and pillow lying on the couch, still in the shape of her husband's body.

'Michael,' she called. His keys and wallet were missing from the hall table. He had already left.

Sophie looked at the yoga mat rolled up in the corner. She had skipped yoga on Monday night because she had forgotten to bring her change of clothes with her and hadn't wanted to bother Rebecca. Besides, after hearing about James, she hadn't been in the mood.

She slipped the DVD into the player and switched on the TV. When she rolled the mat out on the floor, Izzy stopped washing herself and looked up at Sophie. 'It's okay, puss,' she said. 'I'll try not to fall on you.'

Sophie sat in child's pose, her arms outstretched, her forehead pushed into the mat and listened to her breath. A wave of calmness washed over her. The class was easier than Anisha's, just gentle stretches. The twenty minutes flew by. When Sophie lay on her back in Savasana, Izzy sat on her stomach. Sophie laughed and patted the cat on the head. Sophie stayed on the floor for a long time after the DVD had stopped.

When she got out of the shower, she looked at the scales. The number she had seen the day before flashed back into her mind.

'This is bullshit,' she said, to her reflection in the mirror. She put her track pants and singlet back on and took the scales outside. She squared them up with the edges of the pavers, took the top brick from the pile and dropped it on the metal device. The foot area cracked from one side to the other. The second blow shattered the glass in the LCD display. The last blow left a hole exactly in the centre. Sophie picked up the scales and the loose broken pieces and put the lot in the bin.

'I don't know what I am,' she said to the sky, 'but I'm not a fucking number.'

It wasn't until she hung up her towel in the bathroom that she noticed the blood stain. Had she cut herself on the scales? She realised it was menstrual blood. She had started her period, after not having one for months.

She stood in the kitchen, deciding what to eat for breakfast and felt her stomach contract into familiar period cramps. At the same time, she noticed she wasn't hungry. She didn't see any point in eating if she wasn't hungry so she skipped breakfast.

She went to the computer to check out the yoga DVD page on Facebook. The most recent entry linked to a free guided meditation podcast. Sophie clicked through to the website and scanned the titles: *Body Awareness, Simply Being, Emotional Ease, Relaxing into Healing, Letting Go*. She plugged in her iPod and left it to download while she got ready for work.

On the way to the ferry she listened to the first track. The woman's voice was soft and silky, the music a haunting melody. By the time she arrived at work she felt calm and clear-headed. She still didn't know what she should do about the weight she had gained, but for the moment she felt content just waiting to see what would happen.

The park near Beth's house had a playground with a yellow slide, a climbing frame, a seesaw and swings. Max ran ahead and jumped across a set of tyres.

'Don't get dirty,' called Beth. She looked at Sophie and laughed. 'As if that's going to stop him.'

Beth's blond hair curled in soft waves around her face and she wore pale pink lip gloss. She wore a pair of relaxed blue jeans, a white t-shirt and a flowing tie-dyed scarf twisted around her neck. Blue painted toenails peeped out from the ends of a pair of beaded leather thongs.

'Let's start with you,' said Sophie. 'Sit on that bench under the tree and I'll do your head and shoulders. We'll get Max in a minute.'

After a few shots, both Sophie and Beth relaxed. The sun broke out from behind the clouds making the warm afternoon even hotter.

'This is the first time I've ever had a professional

photograph taken,' said Beth. 'I've been meaning to do it for years. I usually take my own photo in the mirror or get Max to have a go. I can't wait to post your photos on my blog.'

Sophie looked surprised. 'Blog?'

'It started out as a record of my lap band surgery but now it's mostly about what Max and I get up to.'

'Hang on,' said Sophie. 'Lap band surgery?'

'Way before I started working at the Opera House, when Max was two. I was overweight before I got pregnant and morbidly obese afterwards.'

'Well it must have worked because look at you now.'

'The surgery had very little to do with it in the end. I lost a shit load of weight the first year, but I put most of it back on. Losing that much weight ravages the body. I couldn't deal with how I looked.'

'What happened?'

'After I regained weight I tried everything to lose it again. I'd lose some then put it back on. Classic yo-yo behaviour. Until one day I read a book about intuitive eating. It took a long time but eventually the weight melted off without me having to do anything.'

'Come on,' said Sophie. 'You must have done something.'

'Yes, I did, but it had nothing to do with food and exercise.'

Max ran across the park and tugged at his mother's arm.

'Can I have a drink, please?'

'There's water in my bag. Once you've had that you can have your photo taken.'

Max screwed up his face.

'How about we do it on the climbing frame,' said Sophie. 'Your mum can stand on the ground and you can climb up behind her.'

'Cool,' said Max.

Sophie could only manage to capture Max's attention for about half an hour before he got bored. She had worked quickly so she had plenty of photos.

'Let's go get ice cream,' said Beth.

'Yay,' yelled Max, and ran to the car.

As Sophie, Beth and Max sat in a cafe spooning cool vanilla ice cream and caramel sauce from their sundaes, Beth continued her story.

'All I can tell you is the two simple things that changed my life. The first is that I learnt to truly believe every woman is beautiful. Every single one. No matter how big or small, how young or old. It's the only thing that matters.'

'But how do you make yourself believe you're beautiful when you look in the mirror and see a body you don't like?' said Sophie.

'You brain-wash yourself. Or more correctly, you de-program yourself.'

Max finished his ice cream and pulled a dog-eared paperback from Beth's bag. He looked at her as if to ask permission and she nodded her head. He sat back down and concentrated on his book.

'I wore a slip-on bracelet around my wrist,' said Beth, 'and every time the voice in my head told me I was ugly or fat or not good enough, I said, out loud if I could, *The sky is blue and my potential is limitless*. Then I'd put the bracelet on the other wrist. By saying something neutral to counteract the negative thoughts, I wore away the neural groove in my brain. And the bracelet was a measure of my progress. I moved it less and less until one day it stayed in the same place all day.

The second thing sounds a bit more woo-woo. It has to do with love. I decided to be the loving person I was looking for in my life. I set out to compliment every person I met, to encourage people who seemed to be struggling, and to be as kind as I possibly could. It was difficult in the beginning so I started out with complete strangers. When my confidence grew I moved on to acquaintances, friends and family. The thing about love is that giving it is as wonderful as receiving it.'

'But what if no one loves you back? What if people take advantage of you?' asked Sophie.

'It happens far less than you might think. It's surprising how people respond differently when you encounter them with a heart full of kindness.' Beth reached out and touched Sophie's forearm. Beth laughed. 'I'm sorry, I've delivered a sermon.'

'Not at all,' said Sophie. 'It's fascinating.'

'Somewhere in the midst of all that self-acceptance and compassion I found a place where I could love myself, sagging skin and all. After that I just followed my instincts and listened to my body. And, well ... here we are.'

'How come I didn't know about any of this?' asked Sophie.

'Because, for the most part, being happy in my own skin is no longer a struggle. Of course, there are bad days, but they don't last. The war is over and I'm living in peace.' Beth's smile seemed to light up her whole face.

'Congratulations,' said Sophie, 'I'm impressed. You've got what most of us only dream about.'

Beth pushed her hair back over her shoulder. 'The thing is Sophie, I'm living proof that it doesn't just have to be a dream.'

CHAPTER NINE

Sophie approached the ferry wharf just as the boat pulled up. She pressed pause on her iPod and pulled the earbuds from her ears. A man, wearing a navy blue uniform, hauled a metal ramp from the deck of the ferry and slid it across to the wharf. Six or seven people got on, Sophie was the last.

She took a deep breath, chanted the word 'love' in her head three times, and said, 'Thank you, sir, you're doing a wonderful job.'

The man nodded his head.

'Seriously, you must have to be strong to haul that ramp on and off the ferry all day. And I bet it's no fun when it's raining. I appreciate all your hard work. Thank you.' Sophie looked into his eyes and gave him her biggest smile.

He smiled back, a faint blush colouring his cheeks. 'You're welcome,' he said.

Sophie sat on the top deck with the smile still on her face. Her chest felt warm and open, her shoulders relaxed. Perhaps Beth was right. Giving out love felt good.

The Stage Door security guard wasn't as easily charmed.

'Good morning, Rex,' she said. She paused before she reached the barricade and turned towards the muscled young man whose left arm was covered in a tattooed sleeve. 'You're doing a fantastic job. Thank you.'

'Sorry?' Rex frowned. 'Did you need something, Sophie?'

'Nothing, except to thank you for making sure all our visitors end up in the right place. And I have no idea how you remember the name of everyone who works here. I'm crap at that.'

'There's a list.' He waved his hand towards the desk.

'Still, it can't be easy. Thank you.' Sophie gave him what she was now calling her 'love smile.' Rex appeared a little confused, but perhaps, Sophie hoped, secretly pleased.

'Okay,' he said, 'I'll get back to it.'

The sight of Jenna's back in the office made Sophie's shoulders contract. It was the first time Sophie had seen her since the Weight Watchers comment.

'Morning, Jenna,' she said. 'That's a nice top.'

'Thanks,' said Jenna, without turning around.

'I'm sorry for snapping the other day, I was in a mood. Weight Watchers has worked for a lot of people — I even tried it once myself. They have a great community and lots of support. Good on you for giving it a go.'

'I lost two kilos,' said Jenna. Sophie felt a surge of anger choke her throat. She couldn't remember the last time she had lost two kilos in a week. Maybe all those years ago when she first started dieting but not anymore. 'Even Jenna, in her polyester blouse, is better than you at losing weight,' said the voice in Sophie's head. *The sky is blue and my potential is unlimited.* She swapped her bracelet from her right wrist to her left.

'Congratulations,' said Sophie. It was all the kindness she could muster.

When Sophie arrived home after yoga, she felt as though she had been rinsed clean from the inside out. When she logged on to her Facebook account, the feeling soon disappeared. Every second post in her news feed was about how much weight someone had lost, how much they had lifted in the gym, their latest 5k run time. One of her friends had posted a picture of herself in her competition bikini. Sophie recognised it as an old photo, taken almost a year earlier. Her friend looked nothing like that now. There were people from the fitness forum posting about their breast enhancements, sponsorship deals and visit to the chiropractor. Two of her friends were awaiting shoulder or knee reconstruction.

Sophie noticed for the first time how much her friends and acquaintances talked about nothing other than their bodies and their physical accomplishments. She sighed and realised she wasn't interested any more. As Pip had said, it was all too intense. Sophie went through her friends list and deleted anyone who had posted a photo of themselves in a bikini or in tight fitting shorts and sports bra. Then she deleted anyone who posted about weight loss. Lastly, she got rid of her subscriptions to any pages relating to health and fitness. As her news feed grew smaller she searched for pages about intuitive eating, meditation, yoga and photography. She was just adding a page about street photography when Michael came home.

Sophie felt the air grow tense. She stood up from the desk and went to kiss him on the cheek. When he pulled away, she exhaled and then smiled her most loving smile.

'If you're not too busy,' she said, 'I'd like to catch up for a few minutes. I've been meaning to talk to you about a few things.'

Michael frowned and put his bag in the study. 'I suppose so,' he said.

She led him to the couch and sat down next to him. She could feel the heat of his thigh a few inches away but they didn't touch.

'It's about my eating disorder and how I think I might have figured out a way to get better. You'll never guess—'

'We talked about this already. You don't have an eating disorder.'

'Okay, but I've been talking to Beth from work and she's put me on to intuitive eating and this exercise where you show kindness to everyone you meet. You should have seen the guy on the ferry this morning. It was amazing.'

'So you think the answer to your problems is to flirt with everyone. I should have known.'

The words stung like a slap to her face. 'Sweetheart—'

'You really can't see it, can you?' He stood up, sweat beading on his forehead. 'I don't want to hear about the guys from Melbourne, or kissing Cristophe Vilas, or anything else you get up to when I'm not around. If you're going to make a fool of me, at least have the decency not to tell me about it.'

'I don't understand...' she said.

'Yes you do. You're a lot of things but you're not stupid.'

'What do you want me to do?'

'Stop flirting or at least stop talking about it. You're embarrassing yourself.' He walked into the kitchen and headed for the fridge. Sophie followed him.

'Michael, I need you to listen. I can't keep fighting with you. It's not what being married should be like. I love you and I want us to be happy. I think we should see a counsellor.' She held her breath, waiting for the explosion.

'If you want to see a counsellor you're on your own.' His voice was barely above a whisper.

'Don't make up your mind right now, think about it.'

'You heard what I said.'

'Do you want to split up?' she said. Michael looked at her. She had never said those words before, not even as a joke.

'No. Do you?'

Sophie started to cry. 'I... no... I don't know...'

Michael cleared his throat. 'Terry and Paul will be here in twenty minutes. We can talk about this later. It's nothing to get upset about. We'll figure it out.' He bent down and kissed her on the top of her head. 'Go wash your face.'

When Sophie saw her puffed eyelids and red eyes in the mirror she started sobbing again. She shut the bathroom door. She turned on the shower so Michael and his friends wouldn't hear her. When her sobs subsided she went into the bedroom. She could hear the sound of Michael and his two friends laughing. She lit a candle, chose the *Letting Go* track on her iPod, lay down on the bed and closed her eyes.

She woke to the sound of Michael's voice.

'I sent them home early,' he said. He sat on the edge of the bed and took her hand. 'I'm sorry,' he said, 'it's been so busy at work. People asking about what books to buy for Christmas. How would I know what stupid little kids read? I didn't mean to take it out on you.'

Sophie sat up and leaned into his chest. He stroked her hair.

'How did we end up like this?' she asked.

'It's just the stress of work, that's all. I don't want to lose you —I love you.'

Sophie looked up and saw tears in his eyes. 'I love you too,' she said.

Michael unbuttoned his shirt, took off his trousers and got into bed. 'Get under the covers,' he said, 'and I'll give you a cuddle.'

They lay together his chest pressing against her spine, his legs behind hers. Soon his hand was on her breast, insistent. She let him make love to her, not moving from the position they were in, the way he preferred it. She wondered if it was because he didn't have to kiss her or look at her face. He pulled out of her before he climaxed, ejaculated against her back and rolled away. She waited until she heard his muffled snores and then went to the bathroom to wash the traces of him from her body.

CHAPTER TEN

That year, she went to the Christmas party. Michael was meant to come with her but he said he had to stay late at work to package up the Christmas orders. She didn't point out that the parcels wouldn't leave until the first post on Monday. She didn't want to start another fight. The studio was decorated with tinsel and a mirror ball hung from the middle of the ceiling. A DJ played dance music in between cabaret performances on the stage. Sophie wore a black dress, the strap from her camera running diagonally across her chest.

Beth arrived with a man who held her hand and looked at her as though he were afraid she would vanish if he looked away. 'This is my boyfriend, Alex,' she said. Sophie kissed him on both cheeks, theatrical fashion.

'You're constantly surprising me,' Sophie said to Beth.

'What other secrets are you hiding?'

'Nothing,' said Beth, and grinned. Alex lifted Beth's hand to his lips and kissed it.

Young men with bare chests carried trays of tiny party pies and prawn balls amongst the guests. Sophie took a party pie and a serviette.

Bruce brought over two glasses of champagne. 'For you,' he said, handing the glass to Sophie. 'I don't think I've seen you at one of these before,' he said.

'No,' said Sophie. 'Even though I've been working here for four years, this is my first.'

'What took you so long?' he asked.

'It's complicated.'

'You should be fine until midnight,' he said. 'And then it gets messy. Watch out for those mechanists — they're a little wild.'

'So I've heard,' said Sophie.

'Gotta go,' said Bruce. 'I'm on in five.'

When the lights came up on stage for the next performance, Bruce stood alone in a spotlight wearing a yellow lame gown and high heels. He had false eyelashes but his face was without makeup, his hair without a wig. He sang a flawless rendition of 'Old Man River' in a deep bass voice while someone in the shadows played a cello. It was strange and beautiful and brought tears to Sophie's eyes. She had been wrong when she had said to Cristophe Velis that Bruce couldn't sing. Entirely wrong. People were showing sides of themselves she never would have expected. Maybe she hadn't been looking hard enough. She took the lens off her camera and took photos of Bruce's curious alter-ego, starting with full body shots and then zooming in on his face. She captured the light in his eyes, the stubble on his cheeks. She captured a slice of time that might otherwise be forever lost.

She spent the evening taking photos of her work colleagues, the ones on stage and the ones around her. She listened more than she spoke and she looked with the eyes of a painter or a sculptor. At midnight, she heeded Bruce's advice and caught a ferry to Milsons Point.

It was a hot night and Sophie was reluctant to go home. She sat on a bench overlooking Lavender Bay, watched the cruise boats sail by and listened to the playful screams from Luna Park. She took a few photos, propping the camera on top of her bag to prevent it shaking during the long exposures. Her bag vibrated. Her phone was ringing.

'I was hoping you were still up,' said James.

'I'm on my way home from the Christmas party,' said Sophie. 'Isn't it a little early for you to be out of bed?'

'Who says I'm out of bed?' he said. Sophie laughed, even though she wanted to be angry with him.

'I've got good news,' he said.

'Yes, I've heard.'

'Wow, Sydney must be a small town. I only found out myself yesterday.'

'Sorry?'

'I've got a gig with the Sydney Festival in January. I fly in to Sydney on New Year's Eve.'

Sophie paused as she adjusted to his news. Her first thought was that he wasn't giving her enough time to lose weight before he arrived. She had been a size smaller when he last saw her. She realised she was being ridiculous. She was still the same person, if anything, a little more relaxed and compassionate.

'Are you bringing your fiance with you?' Her question didn't sound angry. The feeling had slipped out of her grasp.

'No, I'm not.'

Sophie didn't feel like hiding what she felt. It was time to speak openly and honestly, and James was the perfect place to start.

'I didn't know you were with someone until last week when Kim Chen mentioned you were getting married next year.'

'It wasn't a secret. Linda and I have been together for six years.'

'Why didn't you tell me?'

'It didn't think it mattered. You and me, we're just friends, right?'

'Always,' said Sophie. 'But I felt you might have wanted more if I had been willing.'

'Who knows, my darling. We can't live a life of what ifs.'

Sophie leaned back on the bench and looked at the stars. 'It will be good to see you again,' she said.

'So you've forgiven me?'

'Only if you invite me to the wedding.'

'Not likely,' said James. 'We've already 270 on the guest list and the room only holds 250. I can't fit you in.'

'Can you fit me in while you're in Sydney?'

'Damn straight I can. Less than two weeks, Soph. I'll see you soon.'

'Merry Christmas, James. Maybe I'll see you on New Years' Eve.'

'Count on it. I wouldn't want to start the New Year with anyone else.'

Sophie stared at the phone long after James had gone. Luna Park grew quiet and the lights blinked off. She slung her camera over her shoulder, took off her shoes and walked barefoot up the hill.

Want more Sophie Walker?

Sophie's story continues in *Stages | Episode Two...*

December 31st was a hot, sticky day. The forecourt of the Opera House heaved with people, some of them visitors who had no appreciation for the Australian sun, exposing their pale European skin without the protection of sunscreen. Sophie, wearing a halter-neck red dress that skimmed over her hips and plunged between her breasts waited by the entrance, searching the crowd for the sight of James' tousled blond hair. Her heart beat in her throat, perspiration trickling between her shoulder blades. It had been eleven days since she had found out he was flying in from Texas and in that time she had fluctuated between being excited to see him and dreading their meeting. Would he notice that she was heavier, no longer as lean and sculpted as she had been in those first weeks after competing? Would he find her repulsive? She wouldn't blame him.

The tickets to the Lord Mayor's Party lay inside the folds of her purse. She had asked Michael if he wanted to come, but he had brushed the idea away.

'Why would I want to spend an evening with pretentious wankers and D-grade celebrities,' Michael had said. 'I'd rather do something I enjoy. Terry's hosting an all night *Vision Quest* tournament. I'm going over there.'

'You don't mind if I go?' Sophie had asked.

'Go right ahead, if that's your thing.' He must have noticed the hurt look on her face. 'Sorry,' he said. 'I know it's part of your job to brush shoulders with those kinds of people. Enjoy yourself.'

She hadn't told Michael about James — there was nothing to tell. James was a colleague, another part of her job. If any of the cast and crew from any show she'd worked on had been coming to Sydney, she would have done the same thing.

'Sophie. Sophie,' called a male voice with an American accent. James was striding down the hill, waving his arm above his head. He wore a aviator sunglasses and a wide grin. He swept Sophie into a hug with familiarity he hadn't shown before. He held her for a long time, breathing into her hair. She could feel his chest rise and fall against hers, his hand touching the bare skin of her back.

About the Author

Katie Paul used to work in theatre until she had a mid-life crisis and gave it all up to go back to school. She earned her Masters in Non-Fiction Writing and Masters of Creative Writing at UTS.

She teaches Theatre Production to aspiring performing arts students, and writes and self-publishes contemporary women's fiction at Gretel Park Publishing.

gretelpark.com

Other books by Katie Paul

Fiction

Stages | Episode Two
Stages | Episode Three
Stages | Episode Four
Stages | Episode Five
Stages | Episode Six

Non Fiction

The Love Matrix: an unconventional guide to loving yourself

7988025R00062

Printed in Great Britain
by Amazon.co.uk, Ltd.,
Marston Gate.